Maverick Mania

Books by Sigmund Brouwer

SPORTS MYSTERY SERIES

#1 *Maverick Mania*

#2 *Tiger Heat*

#3 *Cobra Threat* (available 8/98)

#4 *Titan Clash* (available 10/98)

LIGHTNING ON ICE SERIES

#1 *Rebel Glory*

#2 *All-Star Pride*

#3 *Thunderbird Spirit*

#4 *Winter Hawk Star*

#5 *Blazer Drive*

#6 *Chief Honor*

SHORT CUTS SERIES

#1 *Snowboarding to the Extreme . . . Rippin'*

#2 *Mountain Biking to the Extreme . . . Cliff Dive*

#3 *Skydiving to the Extreme . . . 'Chute Roll*

#4 *Scuba Diving to the Extreme . . . Off the Wall*

CYBERQUEST SERIES

#1 *Pharaoh's Tomb*

#2 *Knight's Honor*

#3 *Pirate's Cross*

#4 *Outlaw's Gold*

#5 *Soldier's Aim*

#6 *Galilee Man*

THE ACCIDENTAL DETECTIVES MYSTERY SERIES

WINDS OF LIGHT MEDIEVAL ADVENTURES

Maverick Mania

SIGMUND BROUWER

Thomas Nelson, Inc.
Nashville

MAVERICK MANIA

Copyright © 1998 by Sigmund Brouwer.

Published in Nashville, Tennessee, by Tommy Nelson™,
a division of Thomas Nelson, Inc.

Executive Editor: Laura Minchew; Managing Editor: Beverly Phillips
Cover Photo: R. W. Jones / Westlight

Library of Congress Cataloging-in-Publication Data

Brouwer, Sigmund, 1959–
    Maverick mania / Sigmund Brouwer.
       p. cm.—(Sports mystery series)
    Summary: The disappearance of his soccer team's leading scorer
during the championship finals leads sixteen-year-old Matt to
investigate and entangles him in a possible kidnapping.
    ISBN 0-8499-5813-X
    [1. Kidnapping—Fiction. 2. Soccer—Fiction. 3. Mystery and
detective stories.] I. Title. II. Series: Brouwer, Sigmund, 1959–
Sports mystery series.
PZ7.B79984Mav   1998
[Fic]—dc21

                                                98-14576
                                                   CIP
                                                   AC

Printed in the United States of America
99 00 01 02 03 QPV 9 8 7 6 5 4

To Billy Myers, a cool dude—
even if he doesn't play soccer nearly
as well as he writes stories.

One

Fourteen minutes into the first half of our soccer game, a big blond-haired woman interrupted play. Wearing a loose Nike track suit, she ran from the stands onto the field, screaming and waving her arms above her head.

She was being chased by a man with a shaved head who wore a white T-shirt, a red Scottish kilt, and hiking boots. And if all that wasn't bad enough, there was the fact that I knew the man.

He was my dad. And he was trying to yell something over the woman's screaming.

I sighed, spun around, and kicked the ball out-of-bounds to stop the play. It probably wouldn't have mattered. Nobody on the field was thinking soccer anymore, not even the referee. He didn't even bother to blow his whistle. He just stared at the screaming woman.

As for her, she ran like a blind cat with its tail on fire. One of the players from Almont High—our opponent—

was a little slow getting out of her way. I think he simply couldn't believe his eyes. It wasn't until she hit him with a beefy shoulder that he knew it was for real. She sent him tumbling like a bowling pin. Everyone else suddenly decided it was a good idea to make plenty of room for her.

Trouble was, she didn't run in a straight line.

I once saw something like it on a televised rodeo. A bull lumbered around in all directions and ran at the rodeo clowns who were trying to distract it from the fallen cowboy. Just like the bull, this running, screaming woman with flailing arms seemed to aim at the players, who dodged and ducked in different directions so she wouldn't run them over.

And behind her, my dad kept chasing and yelling, with his Scottish kilt flapping around his knees. There were about two hundred fans watching this game, and they were on their feet screaming, too, so it was hard to hear my dad.

The big, blond woman in the Nike track suit stampeded toward my side of the field. As she got closer to me, so did my dad.

I finally heard what he was yelling.

"It's only Larry!" he shouted. "It's only Larry! Slow down! It's only Larry!"

She didn't listen to him. She rumbled past me like a freight train as players wisely scattered.

"Hi, Matt," Dad said, slowing down as he got near me. "Keep up the great work."

"Sure, Dad," I said. Dad's left eye was red and puffy.

I didn't get a chance to ask him about it before he picked up speed again.

"Uh-oh. Watch out," he yelled.

I followed his eyes. The woman had turned around and was headed right back at us, still screaming and waving her arms.

I dove one way. Dad dove another.

She brushed between us and kept on running, arms in the air, high-pitched voice hollering. On my knees, I watched as Dad got up and began to chase her again.

"It's only Larry!" he shouted at her broad back. "It's only Larry!"

I shook my head sadly. This was just another day in the Carr family.

Let me explain my family this way: Dad has a zoo. Mom calls the police at least every ten minutes. My sister surfs in her bedroom. And I'm a sweeper.

But I'm the normal one. Sweeper is the position I play on the Thurber High School soccer team here in Lake Havasu City, Arizona. The way I explain it to people who don't know much about soccer is that I'm like a free safety in football. Our team plays a 4-3-3 formation, with four defenders, three midfielders, and three forwards. I'm the fourth defender, the last guy between the other team and our goalie.

Other things about me: I'm sixteen. My brown hair is not too long, not too short. I don't have a pierced nose or eyebrow or lip. I'm not tall. I'm not short. I wear the kind of clothes that make me look like part of a crowd. I make everybody call me Matt, but my real name is Teague, which is Celtic and means "man of poetry." Just so you get a picture of what I've had to put up with my entire life, there is not a single Celtic person in either my mom's or my dad's entire family history; they just liked the name because it was different. I don't like different. My goal in life, besides playing in the national championship game, is to be normal—unlike the rest of my family.

Mom is a dispatcher for the local police. She's the one who takes incoming calls and radios the messages to the officers in their cars. She applied for the job because she has always dreamed of being a detective, and she's a mystery freak. One entire room of our house is filled with stacks of mystery books. She admits that at forty years old—I know she's lying by three years—she might be too old to become a detective. But she says a person should never stop dreaming. Right now, working as a police dispatcher is the closest thing she can find to reaching her dream.

My sister, Leontine, is fourteen and skinny with bony hips. She wears black everything and actually likes her name and tells everyone it means "brave as a lion." Leontine is an Internet junkie. She surfs the web every possible minute from the souped-up computer in her bedroom. And she has orange-and-purple spiked hair.

Mom, who still wears her hippy clothes from the

1970s, and Dad, who shaved his head because he was losing his hair anyway, both keep telling me that it's what's inside a person that matters. I agree with them in one way—Leontine is a great sister. But in another way, I wish my family could be more like everyone else. When we walk into church together every Sunday—late, of course—I would love it if just once people didn't whisper among themselves as we passed them.

And Dad? He's a sixth-grade science teacher. His students think he's cool—partly because of the earring he wears, partly because he's not afraid of what people think about him. (He plays the bagpipes and wears a kilt when he feels like it, and he isn't even Scottish.) But mostly they think he's cool because he's a great guy who respects his students; he never treats them like little kids.

There's one other reason they like him: his classroom zoo. He's got parrots, a possum, and two iguanas in cages; budgies that fly around while he teaches; and a bunch of piranhas in an aquarium.

What Dad is most proud of, though, is his three-year-old boa constrictor. The snake is six feet long, and Dad says it will someday grow to as long as twenty-five feet. Everyone in the school likes the snake.

Well, everybody except for Freddy, the school janitor. Freddy is terrified of snakes. Even though the boa constrictor lives in a glass cage, Freddy will not step into Dad's classroom to clean unless Dad has taken the snake away.

So, every Friday after school, Dad puts the boa constrictor in a gym bag and takes him out of the classroom for a few hours. This gives Freddy the chance to do his janitor duties.

This was Friday afternoon and, with the final bell, the beginning of spring break. It was also the first day of a weeklong high school soccer tournament. Dad stopped by on his way home from school to watch my team's first game. He must have taken the gym bag containing the boa constrictor into the stands with him.

Did I mention yet that the snake's name is Larry?

Two

I thought for sure that Larry would sleep through the game," Dad said that night at the supper table. "He's only active when he's hungry, and we fed him a mouse on Wednesday. A big mouse, too. It must have taken Larry about an hour to swallow it.

"I'll never cease to be amazed," he continued, "by how Larry eats. He always positions the mouse head-first, so it looks like the mouse is diving into his mouth. Then he swallows, slowly. The last thing you see is the mouse's little tail disappearing—the kids really get into watching that. Then it—"

"Dad?" I said. We were eating spaghetti with meat-balls, long strands of spaghetti that slurped down like mouse tails. I didn't need to be reminded of what I had seen plenty of times. After Larry managed to gulp the mouse whole, the mouse's body slowly moved down the inside of the snake like a tennis ball. Or like a big meatball.

"Yes, Matt?" Dad's left eye was swollen nearly closed. A great big shiner was already starting to show.

"Nothing," I said. He wouldn't understand why I wasn't hungry anymore. I pushed my plate aside.

"Not going to finish?" Leontine asked me.

She didn't wait for my answer before she grabbed my plate.

"Finish your story," Mom told Dad. "And explain your eye."

Our dining room faces the front of the house. Most of Lake Havasu City is built on the side of a low desert mountain that overlooks a valley. Past that you can see a desert mountain range. At the bottom of the valley is Lake Havasu, long and skinny. It runs down the valley for nearly thirty miles. From the table, we had a great view of the reds and browns of the opposite mountains and the incredible clear desert sky as it began to turn purple with the approach of evening.

I concentrated on the view. I didn't want to remember the rest of the story. What I hadn't seen I'd already heard as Dad drove me home from the game.

"Well," Dad said, grinning. Low sunlight from the setting sun bounced off his bald head. "It's probably more Matt's fault than mine."

"What!" I said. "My fault?"

Mom smiled back at Dad. Sometimes it makes me sick how often they give each other goo-goo eyes. Mom's still pretty, I guess. She has long black hair, deep brown eyes, and high cheekbones. Her family is from Mexico. My folks met while Dad was going to

8

college in Los Angeles. I got my dark looks from Mom; Leontine got her looks from Dad's side, the family that came from Norway a couple of generations ago.

"Sure," Dad answered me. "Your fault."

He explained to Mom and Leontine. "Matt was playing such great soccer that I forgot all about Larry, who wasn't as asleep as I thought. Next thing I knew I saw Larry exploring the loose folds of this woman's sweat jacket."

"She was a big woman," I explained, unable to resist. "Just huge. With a really big track suit. Lots of folds."

"The woman was sitting in the stands below you, right?" Leontine said, sucking in a strand of spaghetti like a disappearing mouse tail.

"Exactly," Dad answered. "Larry nosed under the bottom edge of her jacket, so I thought I'd better grab him before he went any farther. I lifted the back of her jacket just as Larry touched her back. She thought it was me. After all, I was leaning down and reaching toward her."

Dad pointed to his left eye. "She turned around quick and punched me hard."

That was about the only part of the story I liked.

"All that movement scared Larry, and he burrowed deeper into the dark safety under her jacket. I tried to get hold of him, but she thought I was grabbing at her again. So she punched me again. Larry took advantage of the confusion to wrap himself around her waist. She stood up and screamed and knocked me over. That's when she realized I wasn't touching her. In a panic, she plowed forward through the people below her. The next thing I knew, she was on the soccer field."

"Oh, my," Mom said.

"'Oh, my?'" I echoed. "She disrupted the game for ten minutes. Running around, she nearly knocked out five players. When she saw the snake's head as it looped up her back and over her shoulder, she fainted. And all you can say is 'oh, my'?"

Dad nodded and added, "Not the least to say how badly it scared Larry. He threw up all over her. Poor snake."

Mom nodded calmly, like none of this was a big deal. Compared to other times, maybe it wasn't. Dad's classroom zoo used to include tarantulas. They escaped—two days before a PTA meeting in the school. They were found . . . in a teacher's purse . . . during the PTA meeting . . . as the teacher reached inside for peppermints.

Mom turned to me. "Matt, you haven't told me how the game went. Did you win?"

"Tied," I said. "No score. Even after overtime."

"That's a bigger surprise than hearing about Larry deciding to explore some stranger's track suit," she said. "Caleb didn't get even one goal?"

"Caleb wasn't there," I said. Our leading scorer had missed the entire game.

"Is he sick?" she asked in concern. She knew as well as I did that only a broken leg would keep Caleb

Riggins away; he would just as soon stop breathing as miss a soccer game.

"That's the weird thing," I said. "Coach called his house and didn't get an answer, not even a machine. I sure hope Caleb shows up for tomorrow's game. If we don't win these early games, we may not make the tournament finals."

"Coach didn't even get an answering machine?" Mom asked. A familiar crazy gleam showed in her eyes. I called it her Sherlock Holmes gleam. Like the one she wore when we followed a car from a gas station here all the way to Las Vegas, about three hours away. Mom was convinced the girl in the backseat kept waving at us because she had been kidnapped. That might not have been so bad, expect Leontine and I were in the car, too, and we needed to get to school.

"The coach called the Rigginses' house and didn't even get an answering machine?" she repeated. "Maybe this is something I should look into. You know his mother never leaves the house. Plus, Caleb's the league's leading scorer, and you guys were expected to sweep your games. This is a big tournament. Maybe somebody on one of the other teams kidnapped him and his family."

I groaned. "Come on, Mom. Caleb just missed one game. Please don't start anything, all right?"

"But Matt . . ."

"No, Mom. Please. *N. O.* No." I let out a deep breath. "I mean, didn't Dad and Larry do enough damage already?

"Besides," I added, "there's no reason to worry. This is Lake Havasu City. Nothing ever happens here. I'm sure Caleb will be at tomorrow morning's game."

I was, of course, very wrong. About Lake Havasu City. And about Caleb.

Three

Saturday morning, I stood behind the sideline at midfield, holding the ball over my head with both hands. This was a crucial throw-in. We were down by one goal, with only twenty minutes left in the game.

While losing the game would not knock us out of the tournament, it wouldn't help our chances. The top eight high school teams in the southwest states—including California and Texas—were here for the round-robin tournament. After every team had played every other team once, the top two would face off in the finals. The winning team would go on to a national tournament, to be televised on ESPN.

I scanned the field. Our team wore blue jerseys. Theirs wore red. No matter how hard I looked, though, I would not see Caleb Riggins. He had missed this game, too.

I looked for an open blue jersey. It wasn't easy. Red

clogged the middle, taking away a direct attack. Red players danced around, covering our blue.

I faked a throw, then saw Steve Martindale break loose on the other side of the field.

Careful, I told myself. Under pressure, it is too easy to make a mistake. I needed to keep both feet on the ground as I threw the ball. It might be routine in practice, but in a tournament, there is no such thing as routine.

Steve stopped, dashed forward, faked a move to the left, then spun back.

I was expecting that. Steve's my closest friend on the team. He's tall, skinny, and has red hair that hangs over his eyes, so he wears a headband when he plays.

I threw, anticipating where Steve was headed. He didn't have to break stride as the ball reached him.

I didn't just stand and watch, though. I sprinted for an open space just behind him. I knew the ball was coming back to me on a give-and-go.

It did.

I trapped it with my right foot.

I knew I had about a second before a red forward was on me.

I pretended to mishandle the ball to give him confidence. It worked. He overcommitted, hoping to strip me of the ball for a clear shot at our net.

I could try my next move only because I knew Steve was ready to back me up and cut the red player off if I lost the ball.

I didn't.

I flipped the ball past the red forward and caught up with it two steps later. Now, briefly, there were ten of us against nine of them.

I kept dribbling ahead. Two reds peeled off to intercept me.

That was all I needed.

Two of my teammates were streaking for open positions upfield.

Time for a killer pass.

I knew I could catch the other team by surprise. All game, I had been hitting first-touch push passes—dumping the ball off immediately with short, safe passes. Not once had I shown the ability to bomb the ball.

I kept my head down, trying to fool them into believing I hadn't seen those two blue jerseys cut past their midfielders.

With a quick flick of my right foot, I served up a forty-yard cross-field pass with some left-to-right spin.

Part of making a pass like this work is knowing your teammates. A lightning fast player will want the ball to land beyond the defenders, so he can zip past them, reach the ball first, and move in to score. A big strong player might want the ball right at his feet. A tall player might want it in the air, so he can knock it down with his chest or head.

As the ball made a banana curve through the air, high above the defenders, I knew I had laid it in perfectly.

Johnnie Rivers, coming in from the right, was a small player, tremendously quick, and he liked getting his passes ahead of him. At this moment, he had the advantage of a full sprint. The ball bounced into an open area just over their sweeper's shoulder. He tried to turn and stay with Johnnie but didn't have a chance.

Because the red defender had been between Johnnie and the goalie as I passed, Johnnie was onside when he reached the ball.

And there were only twenty steps between him and the goalie and the net.

Johnnie, still in full sprint, pushed the ball ahead slightly. He leaned into his kick and beat the goalie clean. And . . . hit the goal post on the left side. The ball bounced harmlessly out of play.

Our hometown crowd groaned.

A clear breakaway. Goalie out of position. And no goal. Caleb Riggins would never have missed a chance like that.

It turned out to be the best shot we had at tying the game.

After that, nothing even came close.

We played out the final minutes, pressing hard. And they still beat us, 3–2.

We badly needed Caleb Riggins's genius scoring touch. But where was he? Why had he missed two games? Why wasn't anyone answering the phone at his house?

Coach had tried calling before and after the game. With no luck. So, with a four-hour break before our next game, I decided to go to Caleb's house myself. That would have been okay . . . except for the dogs.

Four

Steve agreed to go with me. He borrowed his mom's minivan (you might hate to be seen in one, but it's better than walking), and we took off right after the game.

He drove us up McCullough Avenue, which winds up through the city, across, and back down again. The street was named for McCullough—as in chain saws—an industrialist who once flew over the lake and thought it might be a good place to test outboard motors. He set up a mobile home park for the workers and later decided that it was a good place to live. He bought 16,000 acres of desert land on the slopes of the Mojave Mountains overlooking the lake and built a city in the desert. Lake Havasu City grew from zero people to 30,000 in hardly any time.

What most people might know about Lake Havasu City is that the London Bridge was moved here from England. *The* London Bridge—it was taken apart brick by brick on one side of the ocean and put back together here in Lake Havasu City, where it spans a river channel.

"I can't believe Caleb missed two games," Steve said, as he concentrated on the road.

"Without even telling anyone," I added. "Soccer is his whole life. And he knows how much we need him."

"No kidding," Steve said. "The Riverside Mudcats were useless this morning. We should have kicked them so bad . . ."

"Tournament's not over yet," I said.

"Maybe not," Steve answered. "But it will be soon if we don't get Caleb back."

We stopped in front of the house. Number 55 on Desert Quail Drive set at the end of the road. Like most of the houses around, it was built in a southwest adobe style and painted white to reflect the heat. And like most of the surrounding houses, the front yard wasn't grass, but gravel, dotted with desert bushes and a tall cactus. In the summer, Lake Havasu City bakes at more than 100 degrees. Grass takes too much water.

It was a big house. A pontoon boat on a trailer filled one side of the driveway. The boat was big—a flat deck on two cigar-shaped pontoons, with a little cabin on the front to provide shade and a large outboard at the back. It even had a rubber dinghy on the back part of the deck.

Caleb's mom's car, a black Volvo, was parked beside the pontoon boat. His dad's truck, a black Blazer, was behind the Volvo.

This was a family with money. Caleb's dad ran a couple of businesses. He did not shave his head and wear Scottish kilts.

"Check the mailbox," I told Steve as we got out of the minivan. At 11:00, the morning was already getting hot, and because I was still in my soccer uniform, the sun felt good on my bare legs.

"Mailbox?" Steve asked.

"If they've been away for a couple of days, there should be plenty of mail in it."

"None," he said a second later.

"Strange," I said. "And both the cars are here. I wonder why no one's answered the phone."

We walked up the driveway.

No one answered the front door, either.

"They've got to be here," I said. "Unless someone picked them up."

"What if they're outside around back?" Steve asked, pushing his long hair from his eyes.

"Worth a try," I said.

We walked around the house. And stopped in our tracks when two large German shepherds began to bark at us from a kennel. It took us a second to realize they were locked behind the wire fence.

Steve dramatically placed his hand over his heart. "Thought I was dead."

"Me too," I answered. The lawn chairs were empty. The swimming pool was covered. "Safe to say there's no one back here. Unless of course, they're hiding inside and don't want to answer."

The dogs kept barking.

"All right, all right," I told them. "We're going."

We started back toward the front of the house.

"Guys!"

Startled by the voice, we turned back.

"Caleb?" I answered, looking around.

"Right above you."

We looked up and saw Caleb at his bedroom window.

"What's the matter?" I asked. "Coach has been trying like crazy to get you on the phone. We need you big time."

"Yeah," Steve said. "It's a different game without you on the field."

"Win last night?" Caleb asked. He had opened his window and was leaning out, wearing our team track suit. Caleb was medium height, with blond hair. There was a gap between his front teeth, and his eyebrows always seemed arched, like he was asking a question.

"No," Steve said. "Tied. And we lost this morning. The only good thing about the games was when a snake attacked this woman and she ran onto the field."

"What?!"

"Long story, Caleb," I said. "Not worth listening to."

I gave him a puzzled frown. "What's up? Why'd you miss the games? Are you going to be there this afternoon?"

Caleb's face twisted with anger and grief. "I'm grounded."

"Get real," Steve said. "You? Goody two-shoes? Grounded?"

I elbowed Steve. On the way back, he and I would have to have a talk about this thing called tact.

"I was supposed to get all A's," Caleb said. "But I got a B+ in science and that was it. They told me no more soccer."

"But Caleb," I said. "Don't your parents know how important this tournament is?"

He shrugged. Looking closer, I wondered if he had been crying. "They won't let me out of the house."

"Like as if you're in prison," Steve said. "That's not right."

A slight click reached our ears.

Caleb's jaw dropped. He pointed at the kennels.

The latch of the kennel door had somehow opened.

"Guys!" Caleb shouted. "The dogs!—"

But Steve and I were already running. The dogs had pushed the gate open.

To them, we were as tempting as fresh hamburger. They didn't even bother to bark as they bolted straight toward us.

Steve and I scrambled around the corner of the house and ran for the end of the driveway, arms pumping, legs churning.

"The top of the van!" I shouted. "It's our only hope. Climb the van!"

Steve didn't say anything. He was too busy pushing off me to get ahead.

Behind us came the scratch-scratch of dogs' nails scrambling on concrete. Not a nice sound, especially when you're in front of it.

I had almost reached the end of the driveway when I heard a dog's jaw snap closed. At the same time, I felt a hard tug at my shorts. I kept running.

We hit the street and beelined toward the minivan.

Bang! We both slammed into the side of the van to stop our momentum. It was quicker than trying to slow down. Steve nearly pushed my head off as he scrambled up.

I reached the roof of the minivan a few seconds later.

We looked down, expecting to see two vicious German shepherds leaping up at us.

But they weren't even close. They had stopped just at the edge of the yard. They sat there, whining in disappointment at our escape and gazing at us with longing eyes.

I hit Steve in the shoulder.

"Hey," he said. "What was that for?"

"Pushing me back toward the dogs as we ran," I said. "If you were that desperate, why didn't you just flat out trip me?"

"I thought of it," he said. He was panting for breath, just like me. "But I figured it would be worth it only if *both* dogs stopped to get you."

"Jerk," I said.

"That's me." He grinned. "Just remember I've got the keys. And it's a long walk back."

I shook my head. But my mind was already on other thoughts: like, why Caleb's parents were so strict. And how to get Caleb to the next game.

Five

It turned out I didn't have to worry. Five minutes before the afternoon game started, Caleb rode up the field on his mountain bike. He wore an old pair of Nike sweats. After he set the bike down, he jogged toward us.

Because the rest of us had on our team sweats, Caleb stood out from the crowd of players. The guys on our team mobbed him and fired questions and comments as he walked over to meet with Coach Poulsen.

"Where you been, man?"

"Good to see ya."

"We were worried, man!"

"We missed ya, bud. . . ."

Only the coach stayed silent. Mr. Poulsen was extremely tall and extremely thin. He kept his hair bristly short, and it matched his dark brown mustache. Mr. Poulsen wore dark sunglasses, and I couldn't tell if he was angry at Caleb for missing two games.

"Riggins?" was all Coach Poulsen said.

"I need to talk to you, Coach," Caleb said. He looked around at us. "Not a big deal, guys. I just want to explain to the coach."

Earlier, Steve and I had agreed to keep quiet about our morning visit. Caleb sometimes got teased because his parents were so protective. We didn't want to make it worse for him by telling everyone that at sixteen he had been grounded for getting a mark as bad as a B+.

Coach Poulsen and Caleb stepped away from the rest of the team.

I stretched as I looked around. The players on the Phoenix Memorial High Pirates, in green uniforms, were just coming onto the field. Fans filled the stands on both sides of the field. And in the distance, the mountains cut a jagged line against the blue sky of another perfect desert day.

I liked the way I felt. Nervous, but not scared. Inside, butterflies were dancing little circles of excitement, like offstage ballerinas who could barely wait for the music to begin.

My legs felt good, too. Two games in one day was pushing it, but with all the games it took for eight teams to play each other, it couldn't be helped. We'd been practicing and competing all year for this. We still had five games left to make the finals of the tournament, and we had Caleb Riggins back. I was pumped and ready to go.

As we stepped out of our sweats, Caleb and Coach

Poulsen rejoined us. Coach nodded at Caleb, and Caleb peeled off his old Nike sweats to show that he, too, wore our blue uniform.

I didn't think it was strange at the time, but I should have. I just wanted to get a chance to talk to Caleb before the game started.

"Just want you to know," I said, "Steve and I kept it quiet about visiting you this morning. Whatever you tell the team is fine with us."

"Thanks," Caleb said. "About the dogs—"

Coach Poulsen called for a team huddle.

"Later," I told Caleb. "We've got a game to win."

He grinned.

It was good to have him back.

Twenty minutes into the second half, we faced our biggest challenge. We were up 1–0, thanks to an early goal by Caleb. He had taken a pass from a corner kick by Steve and bounced it just under the crossbar of the net with his head.

Nobody could head the ball better than Caleb. When I asked him about it once, he told me it was simple: He pretended he was throwing his eyes at the ball as he jumped at it.

As the game wore on, that one goal began to look bigger and bigger. If our defense held, we would win the game. And, so far, our midfielders had done such a great job of clogging the center line that we had not been pressed once.

Now, though, as two of the green played a tricky give-and-go, Johnnie ran into Steve and both of them fell. The greens took the opportunity to swarm into an open gap in our territory.

I watched carefully.

We played a man-to-man defense; Coach Poulsen had told us early in the season he would give us that freedom as long as we could prove it worked better than a zone defense. So far, it had. But now Steve and Johnnie lay in a tangle, way behind the play.

As sweeper, I didn't have anyone specific to guard. Last man back, I could see most of the field. My job was to anticipate dangerous plays and stop them.

Their striker—one of the forward attackers—was a tiny redhead, quick as a hummingbird. I figured they would try to get the ball to him.

He began to edge toward the sideline, staying just ahead of me to remain onside.

I watched their midfielders pass the ball back and forth, advancing it so quickly that Steve and Johnnie couldn't catch up to them.

Then it came!

The same bomb play that I had tried the day before.

Their redheaded striker was bursting toward the center. One of the midfielders booted a high, hard pass.

I didn't make the mistake of going for the ball. It was too big a risk. By chasing it, I would have taken myself on a diagonal line away from the center of our net. If I missed it, their striker would have a short, clear shot.

Instead, I turned my back on the ball and focused on the tiny redhead. The ball was just behind him, and he had to take a half-step hop to slow himself down. I slid and hooked my foot, stopping the ball as he overran it. I hopped up, spun around, and looked upfield.

Riggins!

He was a blue blur, already near their sweeper, who had been just a little too confident about their forward press.

Without even thinking, I snapped a hard kick, putting my whole body into it. When the ball landed, it was ahead of Caleb by about ten steps, but he was in full sprint and reached it with a three-step lead over the nearest green player.

The rest of the play seemed to run in wonderful slow motion.

Caleb dribbled the ball without losing speed, held it long enough to force the goalie deep into the net, then picked an easy wide-open corner.

The net bulged. The hometown crowd went wild. And we were up 2–0.

I'd held my breath while watching; I finally sucked in some air.

The redheaded striker on the other team stood beside me.

"Nice block," he said. "And nice pass. You guys deserved that goal."

"Thanks," I answered. With so little time left, the game was almost ours.

"Too bad about your shorts, though," he said as he trotted away. "Aren't you afraid of a sunburn?"

I stared after him, puzzled. Then I reached around behind me. And discovered a not-so-good thing.

It had probably started when the dog had nipped my shorts in Caleb's driveway. And my slide apparently hadn't helped. When I reached behind me, I discovered a very big hole in the back of my shorts.

I stood there, worrying about how to get off the field without showing the entire world a part of my body that my mother had powdered when I was a baby. Before I could move, Caleb's father walked up to the field from the parking lot.

He was a big man with a dark beard, dressed in a dark blue three-piece suit. He put two fingers in his mouth and whistled.

Caleb looked over, dropped his head, and slowly trotted to the sidelines.

Although there were still five minutes left in the game, Mr. Riggins grabbed Caleb by the elbow and took him away.

Because everyone was watching them, I was able to get to the bench and put on my sweats unnoticed. But it suddenly seemed that ripped shorts were a pretty minor problem.

Six

"**C**an a parent do that?" I asked at the table during our evening meal. I had just explained to Mom what had happened to Caleb. "I mean, it was like Mr. Riggins thought he owned Caleb. If anyone else had dragged Caleb away like that, it would have looked like kidnapping."

Dad pushed his food—some kind of casserole— around on his plate. Because my folks both work, Mom insists that Leontine and I each make dinner once a week. It was Leontine's turn to torture us, and everyone, including Mom, was too afraid to ask about what we were eating.

"Well," Dad said, "it did look unfair. But there might be a lot you don't know about the situation. I think it's wrong to judge. For all you know, Caleb lied to you about why he was grounded. And it looked to me like Caleb had disobeyed by going to the soccer game. He wore old sweats to hide his uniform and rode to the field on his bike instead of getting a lift. You know his dad always drives him to games."

"But legally, can't Caleb do something?" I mushed my food, trying to make it into smaller pieces that I could hide under a piece of bread. I hoped the phone would ring and Leontine would answer it. That would give me a chance to dump my dinner back into the casserole dish. "How can they stop him from playing soccer?"

"He's not eighteen," Dad said. "I believe the law would still consider him a minor and under his parents' care."

"I know there's something mysterious about all of this," Mom said.

"Do you like the casserole?" Leontine asked me.

"It's an interesting flavor," I said. *Interesting* is a good, nonspecific word. The casserole was horrible, in an interesting way. "Is that a new streak of green in your hair?"

All it takes to distract Leontine is to get her talking about her hair or her clothes.

"Oh, yes," Leontine said. "Me and my friends had nothing to do today, so we—"

"My friends and I," Dad corrected her. "What you do is take away 'my friends' and see whether 'I' or 'me' works by itself. You wouldn't say, 'Me had nothing to do today.' You would say, 'I had nothing to do today.' Then add your friends to the sentence, and it comes out, 'My friends and I had—'"

"Listen," Mom said from her end of the table, "I really did find out something that makes this a mystery."

She says that a lot. Last month, she was convinced

that one of our neighbors—old Mr. Cardston—was a Nazi war criminal. The embarrassing part was when he caught her stealing his garbage to look for letters from other Nazi war criminals.

Dad rubbed his bald head with both hands. He tells us he does it because the stubble itches where he's shaved his scalp. But Leontine and I have noticed he only does it when he doesn't want Mom to see him smirk at another one of her crazy ideas.

"Yes, dear?" Dad asked mildly.

"On my way to work today," Mom said, "I drove past the Rigginses' house. I took down their license plate numbers and got some of my police friends to check them out. I spent the rest of the day asking questions and learning everything I could."

Dad began to rub his scalp harder. "Yes, dear," he said again.

Mom was so excited about her detective work, she didn't notice his lack of enthusiasm.

"First of all," she said, "the Rigginses moved here about thirteen years ago when Caleb was only three."

Dad whistled. "Lock them up."

Mom frowned at him. He smiled sweetly, like a little boy caught with his hand in the cookie jar.

"You were saying . . . ," he said.

"The thing is, there is a weird gap in their credit record. It's like they stopped living for the year before they moved to Lake Havasu City. How do you explain that? Then, when they resurfaced, they had a lot more money."

"Must be part of the Mafia," Dad said. "I bet he used to own half the mob in New York. He moved here to get away from them and lives under an assumed name."

Mom looked at him with a thoughtful expression.

"I was just joking," Dad said quickly. "Maybe he inherited a fortune. Or won a lottery. There could be any of a dozen explanations."

"Uh-huh . . . I'd like you to do me a favor. You have keys to the school, right?"

Dad nodded. He looked like he had heartburn, but I knew he hadn't touched any of the casserole. So it must have been from Mom's need to find a mystery in everything.

"Check the school files," Mom told him. "Caleb is a year ahead of Teague—"

"Matt," I said. "Please, it's Matt." I live in dread of the day she'll call me "Teague" in front of my friends.

"Caleb is a year ahead of Matt in school," Mom told Dad. "Surely there's something in the grade school records about Caleb."

Dad finally sighed. "I'm not sure it's right to do that. It's not public information and—"

"There's one thing I didn't tell you," Mom said. Her voice became quiet. "There's a police file on Charlie Riggins. And it makes me really sad."

We waited.

"Twice the police were called to his house for a domestic disturbance."

"What!" Dad said.

"His wife never pressed charges, but he hit her," Mom answered. "And a man who will hit his wife might also hit his son."

Seven

The next day, Sunday, was a tournament break day. Every team had played three of its seven games. With one win, one loss, and one tie, it looked like our Thurber Mavericks would need to win at least three out of the next four games to place in the top two and make the finals of the tournament.

As usual, my family went to church. As usual, I was the only one dressed normally. And, as usual, I excused myself to go to the bathroom as soon as we got to the church. I hoped that Mom and Dad and Leontine would go ahead and find a place to sit without me. But, as usual, they waited for me to return.

So, as usual, I took a deep breath and walked in with them—a sister with more colors in her hair than her clothes, a father with a shaved head and an earring, and a mother who made sure to stop and greet everyone as we walked up the aisle.

Once we were seated and I knew that nobody was

staring at us, I relaxed and started thinking church stuff. I've learned from Dad that there is a big difference between faith and religion. Faith, he told me, is a matter of the heart, of getting close to God. I like remembering that. While some of the people sitting in the pews might be real jerks away from church, it doesn't mean that what I learn in church is as phony as they are.

We have a good preacher who uses stories to help us understand the message, and most Sundays I pay close attention. Today, though, my mind kept wandering, no matter how hard I tried to listen. I kept thinking about Caleb. Not because I was worried about our soccer team. (All right, not *mainly* because of soccer.) But because I kept seeing him, in my mind, getting dragged away by his father.

It didn't seem right or fair. What could kids do if their parents weren't good parents? Mine might dress and act strange, but at least they always treated me with love.

The more I thought about it, the more I worried about Caleb.

As church ended, I decided I would head up to Caleb's house . . . without a plan.

As it turned out, I could have used one.

Eight

I was sweating hard by the time I made it up McCullough Avenue to the turn for the Rigginses' house. Without Steve and his mom's minivan, I had to rely on leg power and my mountain bike. At the corner, I stopped to take a drink from my water bottle.

Below me, in the valley, I saw the glint of Lake Havasu and its beautiful blue against the desert reds and browns. I thought of how nice it would be on the lake's beach. And I nearly turned around.

What kept me from heading to the lake, though, was thinking of how miserable Caleb might be. *What if his father did hit him? If the situation were reversed,* I reminded myself, *I'd want someone to try to help me.*

I gulped some more water, trying to talk myself out of going up to the house. Then into it. Then out of it again.

I told myself I would just ring the doorbell. If Caleb answered, I would ask him how he was doing. If his mom or dad answered, I would pretend I didn't know anything about Caleb's trouble. I would invite him to join me for a bike ride. It wasn't much of a plan, but it was the best I could come up with.

When all my water was gone, I had no more excuses to stand there. I hopped on my bike and pushed ahead.

What I found was the last thing I had expected. I'd worried and worried about what I would do if Mr. or Mrs. Riggins answered the door. But when I got close to his house, the Blazer was gone. As was the Volvo. And the pontoon boat.

The shutters on the windows were closed completely. It looked like the Riggins family had gone on vacation.

Except for the dogs.

As I rode up to the driveway, I changed to a lower gear. The sound of my bicycle must have alerted them. They trotted around the side of the house, curious about the noise. When they saw me and my bicycle, they barked and dashed forward.

Without much of a head start, I knew I was in trouble.

To spin my bike around, I braked my rear wheel hard and cranked my front wheel, sliding my right foot on the pavement to keep my balance. Even before I had turned completely, the dogs were halfway down the driveway.

I stood on my pedals and started to push with all my strength.

And my stupid bicycle chain snapped.

It was so sudden, I fell forward, nearly banging my chin against my handlebars.

What stopped me, however, was my lower body. It connected with the crossbar of the bicycle. In that split second, I wished as hard as I could that I rode a girl's bike.

I toppled over and my bicycle landed on top of me.

I could not have been more helpless—tangled up in a mountain bike, in total agony, with two snarling dogs closing in on me.

Nine

At the end of the driveway, the dogs stopped short. Almost as if someone had yanked them from behind by their collars.

Their fierce barking turned to whines. They paced back and forth across the end of the driveway, just like lions in a cage—with invisible bars.

I didn't understand.

All they had to do was come a few feet off the property, and they could rip me apart. What was stopping them? Were they so well trained that they wouldn't go past the end of the driveway, no matter how tempting their prey?

I groaned as I pushed the bike off me. I felt so bad that I nearly wished the dogs had managed to bite me. Kind of like wanting to whack your thumb with a hammer to take your mind off a toothache.

The dogs whined louder as I backed away. Drool hung from the sides of their mouths as they panted.

"Too bad, guys," I told them. "You'll have to find someone else to eat. Like maybe Little Red Riding-Hood."

I steadied my bicycle. The good news was that going home was all downhill. I wouldn't have to walk the bicycle home. I took a few deep breaths and finally felt like I might live.

I began to push my bike away from Caleb's house.

The dogs followed me along the edge of the property as far as they could.

"Good riddance," I told them, looking back and sticking my tongue out at them.

That's when I noticed it. Tucked beneath the collar of the bigger dog was a folded piece of paper. The ends stuck out of each side of the collar.

A note?

I studied both dogs, wondering again what kept them on the Riggins property. But I wondered even more about the piece of paper.

If it was a note, it had to be from someone the dogs trusted. I doubted either dog would let a stranger get close enough to touch its collar. So it had to be from someone in the Riggins family. Surely not Mr. Riggins, he would have no reason to leave a note behind.

Caleb?

The more I thought about it, the more I felt sure he had left a message for someone who might come to the house looking for him.

But why? He hadn't been kidnapped or anything. Parents don't kidnap their own kids.

Or do they? And if they did, why?

I wished the dogs could talk. Much as I wanted to read the folded piece of paper, I wasn't stupid enough to reach over and tempt those long yellow fangs.

The dogs and I stared at one another for a few more minutes. I finally walked my bike to the end of the street, got on, and began to coast down McCullough Avenue toward home.

Warm wind filled my face. The view of the valley below filled my eyes. And questions filled my mind.

Somehow, I needed to see that note.

Ten

That night, Steve picked me up just after eight in his mom's minivan. I had until eleven to return. Mom and Dad have rules they expect me to follow, and I've discovered life is much easier when I respect them because my parents return that respect and trust me.

Steve took us up to McCullough Avenue. The smell of hamburgers filled the van from the paper bag beside Steve. And it took me less than ten seconds of squirming to find out I had sat on a Barbie doll. That's the disadvantage of family vehicles.

"You're sure the burgers won't kill them?" I asked, digging the doll out from under me.

"Dad and I did the math," he answered. "For what the dogs weigh, and with the strength capsules we're using, Dad said they would be fine. There are only four in each burger."

Steve's dad is a doctor. He had only given us approval for this after listening carefully to our plan

. . . and after deciding we weren't breaking any laws. Steve's dad had seen Caleb get hauled out of the soccer game, too, and was as worried as we were.

"Good," I said.

Neither of us said much more as we drove up McCullough. We'd already gone through everything that afternoon when I called Steve with this plan.

We stopped a couple of blocks away from the street where the Rigginses lived. We didn't want anyone to see the van.

"Ready?" Steve asked me.

"No," I said.

"No?"

"Like, is anyone ever ready for a dentist appointment?"

"Good point," he said.

We got out of the van. He carried the hamburger bag. I carried a pair of gloves and a heavy jacket.

We walked down the street. Here, in the upper part of the city, we were far away from the London Bridge and all the little shops along the boardwalk near it where tourists go. Lake Havasu City has a lot of older, retired people, and we've always joked that everyone but the tourists goes to sleep right after dinner.

It could be true. No cars passed us. Many of the houses were dark except for porch lights.

Even though I was nervous, I couldn't help thinking my usual thoughts about desert nights. It's the stars, actually. In the desert, especially out in the hills away from the city lights, the big stars seem to poke bright holes in the sky and the little stars look like white dust blown in all directions. When I start to think about where the stars came from, I start to think about God.

What messes with my mind is knowing that it's impossible for something to come from nothing. I mean, little rocks don't just appear from thin air. They come from bigger rocks. Bigger rocks come from boulders. And boulders come from mountains. And mountains come from the earth. If you go back far enough, the earth must have come from the same stuff that made the stars.

But if you go even farther back, where did the stuff to make the earth and the planets and the billions and billions of stars come from?

It couldn't have come from nothing.

And it couldn't just simply exist. Go as far back as you want in time, and you still have to have a starting point for the stuff that made the planets and the stars.

So when I look at the stars, I realize there has to be a God that created the first something. And I wonder about what he intended for us to do with our planet and whether we're listening hard enough to his plan.

"Hey," Steve said. "Looking for UFOs?"

I had been staring at the sky as we walked.

"Something like that," I said, hiding a smile. There were times to talk serious and times not to. This was a time not to.

We had a job ahead of us. A dangerous job.

The first part was easy. The Riggins house was by itself at the end of the street. It was dark and quiet.

The Blazer and the Volvo and the pontoon boat were still gone. The windows were still shuttered. There was nobody to bother us as we whistled for the dogs from the sidewalk.

As before, they came bolting around the corner of the house, a pair of dark wolflike shadows.

"You sure they'll stop?" Steve asked.

"They did twice before," I said. "Like there's a glass wall at the end of the driveway."

Still, I was nervous. I didn't breathe until the dogs stopped just short of us. They kept growling as they eyed us. It sounded like the rumbling of a volcano.

Steve pulled a small flashlight from his back pocket. He flicked it on and pointed it at the dogs. The beam of light showed that the folded paper was still under the collar of the bigger dog.

"Just like I told you," I said. "And I don't think the dog put it there."

"And you figure it's worth all this?"

"What's the worst that can happen?" I asked him in return, pretending I hadn't thought about police, or the Rigginses coming home, or . . .

Steve waved the hamburger bag. It got the dogs' attention.

"Good doggies," Steve said as he reached into the bag. "Good, hungry doggies."

He tossed them each a hamburger. The burgers only lasted one or two seconds. Which was about how long Steve and I would last if they decided to leave the property and come after us.

45

"You said four in *each* burger," I said to Steve. "Right?"

Looking at how big the dogs were, I hoped Steve and his dad had calculated correctly.

"Four sleeping pills per dog," he said. "Trust me, they're about to take a nice little trip to la-la land."

Eleven

It took about twenty minutes for the dogs to take their nice little trip to la-la land. If I hadn't been so worried about Mr. Riggins driving up at any second, I would have found it funny.

First, the dogs stopped pacing at the end of the driveway. Then, slowly, the dogs sat. Then they rolled sideways to stretch out. Their growls became snuffling.

Steve used a small flashlight to check them. Neither dog opened its eyes at the light.

I wanted to give them five more minutes to be sure, but Steve wanted to grab the note and get going. He pointed out that I had my jacket and gloves to protect myself.

"Yeah, yeah," I said. "Here are the jacket and gloves. You do it."

"Your idea," he said. "And you're the one who thinks it's a note from Caleb. I'd hate to do all the work and discover *you* were wrong."

"Fine," I said, using the one word that means just the opposite.

I took a half step onto the driveway, ready to jump back if the dogs moved.

Nothing but snores.

I moved closer. Very scared. Even with the heavy jacket and gloves, I knew the dogs were big enough to shred me if they woke.

Nothing but snores.

Steve beamed the flashlight on the dog's collar. I saw a little sensor box attached and finally understood why the animals never left the property. It was called invisible fencing. The sensors on the dogs' collars gave them little shocks if they moved past an electric "fence" that circled the yard. That meant Mr. Riggins could let them roam free to guard the property.

But Mr. Riggins hadn't planned on the special hamburgers.

I leaned down, close enough to smell the dog's hamburger-and-onions breath. I gave a slight tug and pulled the paper free. The dog snorted and flinched but remained asleep.

I backed away, my eyes glued to the dogs.

Two steps later, I stood on the sidewalk beside Steve.

"Open it up," he said. "What's it say?"

"Let's get out of here first," I said, tucking my gloves in my back pocket.

We walked as fast as we could back to where we'd parked the minivan.

I waited until we were driving away to turn on the interior light and unfold the paper.

I'd been right. It was a note from Caleb.

I don't know how long we'll be gone. I don't even know if we'll be coming back. I pray that someone finds this note. Please look for me. And whatever my father says, don't believe him. I have to go now. He's outside my bedroom door waiting for me. If I don't do what he says, he hits me.

Caleb Riggins

I read the note out loud to Steve.

He whistled a long, low note. "Doesn't sound good, does it?" he said.

"No," I answered. "It doesn't sound good at all."

Twelve

Monday morning turned out to be one of those rare days in Lake Havasu City when it rained. Or at least, rained by our standards. To people from anywhere else, the light misting of water would have counted not as a rainstorm but as a slight bother.

It didn't stop our scheduled soccer match at nine that morning. There was a stiff wind, and gray patches of clouds scudded across the sky. I shivered and stamped my feet as I waited for the coin toss that would decide who kicked off to start the game.

Steve stood beside me. The wind pulled at his long hair.

"No sign of Caleb," he said.

"Are you surprised?" I asked.

"No."

"Me neither," I said. "My mom has the note. She's taking it to work this morning to ask her police friends what to do."

"We need him pretty bad," Steve said.

"Yeah," I said. I hadn't slept much during the night, worrying about all the things that the note could mean. "I just hope he doesn't need us worse."

Because we were hometown favorites, most of the couple hundred people in the stands were cheering for us, including my dad, with a bright blue-and-green parrot on his shoulder. Even though the school was closed for spring break, Dad had stopped by this morning early enough to do some work and pick up his favorite animal from the classroom zoo, Petey the Parrot.

Most of the people around Dad probably didn't think seeing a forty-year-old man with a shaved head, an earring, and a parrot was too strange—but only because they had known our family long enough to expect crazy things.

When the Camille High Cougars in their orange jerseys scored their first goal against us five minutes into the game, all the hometown fans started yelling at the referee for missing the offside call that led to the goal.

To me, there was no doubt the referee should have called their striker offside. As sweeper, I had been easily three steps behind him. A tall guy with short blond hair, he had been waiting between me and the goalie before the pass reached him. Offside. But the ref had not blown his whistle, and the striker had dribbled twice and kicked the ball into the high corner of the net.

Our goalie, Stew Schmid, had begun to run toward the referee to complain. I stepped in front of Stew to stop him. About my height, he wore glasses now covered with small drops of rain.

"Bad break," I told Stew. "Goal shouldn't count."

"Goal shouldn't count? Of course the goal shouldn't count!" Stew tried to push me out of the way. "Let me at that ref. He's going to hear it from me. Then I'm going to flatten his nose. And after the game, I'm going to flatten his tires. If we don't score, that call might cost us the tournament and a shot at the televised nationals."

I knew Stew was right. When soccer games are decided by only one or two points, every goal is crucial. Without Caleb to pour them in for us, this goal against us might be even more crucial. And from here on in, we had to win every game. Even a tie might take us out of the final two spots.

But I also knew a couple of other things. If Stew stayed worked up and angry, he was going to have a hard time concentrating for the rest of the game. If I let him past me to argue with the ref, Stew could blow the anger out of his system. If not, we might be down another couple of goals before the end of the half.

On the other hand, the ref wasn't going to change his mind no matter how much anyone argued with him. It would only make the situation worse to have him mad at us. And if Stew really let loose, he might get kicked out of the game.

"Stew," I said. He was staring over my shoulder, watching the referee take the ball to the center for another kickoff. "If you had five shutouts in a row and not one person said you were doing great, what would you think?"

"Be a little mad," he said. "Like I am now."

"And what if, after all those perfect games, everyone jumped on you for your first mistake?"

"Be even madder," he said.

"That's what it's like for refs," I said. "Nobody notices their good work. I hate the call as much as you do. Later, he might even tell us he made a mistake. But he's refereed other games for us, and he's usually good. Only thing is, people don't tell him. All they do is notice his mistakes. If we give him a break now, he might give us a break later."

Stew was starting to calm down.

"Besides," I said, grinning. "See the guy's legs? They're so pasty and skinny, it looks like he's riding a chicken. You've got to feel sorry for someone who goes public with legs like that."

Stew finally laughed.

"All right, all right," he said. "I'll give him a break. But next time . . ."

"Won't be no next time," I promised. "And we're going to win. Just wait and see."

Five minutes later, Stew scooped up a ball that was rolling across his crease. He threw it ahead to me. I found Johnnie open at midfield, and lofted him a pass.

He made a move to get past two defenders, found some room, and sprinted. Two of our strikers stayed with him, and just like that, we had three attackers against two defenders.

With the crowd cheering and screaming for us, our three guys advanced the ball to pull a gap between the defenders. One pass. Two. Three. When the ball came back to Johnnie, he faked the fourth pass and laced the ball with a perfect kick that hit the inside of the right post and crossed the goal line.

Tie game!

Five minutes after that, with our guys swarming their zone, Johnnie broke past their sweeper on a play that was so close to offside the ref could have called it either way.

The ref let it go, and Johnnie flicked his foot to direct the ball into the upper left corner. The net bulged.

Two–one, Mavericks!

I thought back. If Stew had yelled at the ref earlier, the ref might have been mad enough to call the offside against us. Maybe because we kept our cool, the referee decided to give us a break and let the close call go our way.

At that moment—even though he was sitting in the stands with a parrot on his shoulder—I was glad for Dad's advice over the years. He'd been the one to show me the game from the ref's point of view. He'd also often reminded me that in the history of soccer, while time and again people blamed the ref for losses, no one had ever won a game and given the referee credit.

The score stayed 2–1 for us.

At the end of the game, when we walked off the field, we still had a chance at making the finals. And at the televised nationals beyond that. But we had to keep winning. And our chances would get slimmer and slimmer without Caleb to help us in the next few games.

Thirteen

In the kitchen at lunchtime, Dad hung up the phone.

"Your mother sounded frustrated," he said. "And if she is frustrated . . ."

At the counter, knife dripping with mustard in one hand, I knew what he meant. Mom sees the bright side of everything.

I smeared the mustard on bread. It was my turn to make the meal. A person could never go wrong with sandwiches.

"What did she say about the note?" Leontine asked from the dining room. She was at the table playing a computer game on her laptop. "Are the police going to do anything about it?"

"That's why she's frustrated," Dad answered. "There's nothing they can do."

Irritated, I slapped the last of the sandwiches together and put them on a tray. "Didn't they read what Caleb wrote? Anybody can tell he's in trouble.

And he didn't show up this morning for the game. Doesn't that mean anything?"

I carried the tray to the dining room. "If you can't go to the police for help, where do you go?"

Dad joined Leontine and me at the table.

"What a surprise," he said. "Sandwiches."

"Sarcasm is not a pretty thing, Dad," I said.

"Let me guess," Leontine said, joining the attack from the other side. "Ham and cheese with mustard and lettuce."

"At least you can guess what it is," I answered.

"And what is that supposed to mean?" she asked. "If you didn't like my casserole, just say so."

"Oh," I said, grinning. "Casserole. Thanks for the hint."

"Guys, guys," Dad said. "I'd rather hear someone say grace than start World War Three."

Leontine said grace, and we began to eat.

"About the note, Dad . . . ," I prompted him.

"A couple of things," he said. "The police can't act on the note because they can't be sure it was Caleb who wrote it."

"He signed his name!" I said.

Dad shrugged. "The police say it could have been written by anyone. Second, even if it was Caleb, they say he might be making things up to get attention. And third, Caleb is still a minor. No one can stop his parents from taking him wherever they choose. If Caleb is not back by the time school resumes next week, there might be some legal action the police can take."

"That's dumb," Leontine said, looking up from her computer. She had a sandwich in one hand and was typing with the other. Mom would never let her get away with it, but she knew Dad and I liked to read during meals. Whenever Mom had to work, our lunches were pretty quiet. Except, of course, for this one.

"I agree," I said. "The police have those reports Mom told us about. About how Mr. Riggins hit his wife. They should at least look into it."

"What I just gave you were the official answers Mom got," Dad said. Mustard was streaked across his cheek. "Unless the Rigginses put Caleb in physical danger, the police have their hands tied in terms of any legal action they can take. But unofficially, they have promised to look for them. It's the best they can do."

"I see why Mom is frustrated," I said.

"Maybe there's something Leontine can do," Dad told us. He dug into his back pocket and pulled out some papers. "I picked this up at school this morning."

Dad handed the papers to me. The first page was a photocopy of school registration information when the Rigginses had first brought Caleb to school way back in first grade. There was also a photocopy of Caleb's birth certificate.

"It's not much to go on," Dad said. "It just confirms what your mother said earlier. That they moved here when Caleb was three. The only new thing is that it looks like they came from a town called Roaring River in North Carolina."

"Long ways away," I said. "And a long time ago. What can Leontine do with that?"

"Something on the Internet," Dad said. He looked at Leontine, who was nodding. "Maybe there's a way to get to local newspapers. Or maybe you can hook up with a local chat group. I looked up Roaring River on a map. It's a very small town. Surely someone there would remember the Riggins family. It will simply be a matter of finding someone on the Internet who lives there."

Dad shrugged again. "For now, it's the best that we can do."

The mustard on Dad's face was driving me nuts. I went to the kitchen, found a cloth, rinsed it with warm water, brought it back to Dad, and pointed at his face.

"Hate to have you looking strange," I said. I wondered if he would catch my sarcasm. I was always bugging Dad about his earring and the way he dressed.

"Thanks," he said, ignoring my remark as he wiped away the mustard.

He washed down the last of his sandwich with milk. "One other thing," Dad said. "Something the school librarian told me when I went back after the game to return Petey to his cage."

"Mrs. Kappa?" I asked.

"Yup. She taught first grade before taking over the library. She had Caleb in one of her classes. I saw her in the hallway and asked if she remembered anything about him. She did. But it may not mean anything."

"Fire when ready," I said.

"She said he wrote a story about having a twin brother on a golden bridge. The story itself didn't get her attention. She says lots of kids that age have imaginary friends in fairy-tale places. What struck her, though, was the way his father reacted when she showed him the story during a parent-teacher conference. She said Mr. Riggins got really angry at Caleb for making up lies. She said that Caleb missed the next two days of school, and when he did come back, he was quiet and withdrawn."

Dad looked out the window, talking more to himself than to us. "Back then, a teacher never suspected that a parent would hurt a child—physically or emotionally. It's sad to say, but now, we have to be more concerned with such things."

He sighed. "The world seems a lot less innocent now. I wonder if poor Caleb got hit for making up his story."

"I can't believe that a grown-up would hit a little kid," I said. "Especially over something like a make-believe story."

"It happens," Dad said. "Worst thing is, the kid falsely believes it's his fault. But usually the parent has just redirected anger over problems he or she is facing."

"But what kind of problem could Mr. Riggins be facing?" I asked. "He's one of the most respected businessmen in the city."

"I imagine," Dad answered, "that when we learn the answer to that, we'll learn why Caleb wrote that note."

Fourteen

Because so few points are scored in soccer, just one goal can make a tremendous difference in the game's outcome.

That afternoon, we just needed one goal against the Sylvan High Eagles. The score was 1–1, and only ten minutes remained in the game. The Eagles' defense was as tight as ours. Whoever scored next would probably win.

Trouble was, they played zone defense so well that one of their yellow jerseys always seemed to move into place to block our passes.

This late in the game—and knowing we had to win this game to keep our tournament chances alive—it seemed smart to take a few risks.

If I could somehow beat one or two of their guys, the field would open up and crack their zone defense.

I waited for the ball to come back to me. The morning's light showers had passed over the valley, and now sunshine in a clear sky dried the sweat on my face. Although I was concentrating on the game, I was aware of the crowd's cheering. Sometimes it goes like that. When you concentrate hard on one thing, all your other senses become more keen, too.

I watched my teammates upfield, trying to store their positions in my memory. When Johnnie ran into a defensive wall and had to pass back to me, I was ready.

I hung on to the ball instead of passing it off quickly as I had done all game. As I moved up the field, a yellow jersey cut into my line of vision.

I had to decide quickly. Was this real pressure or panic pressure?

Sometimes players see attackers and panic makes them react too soon. It's only real pressure when the attacker is close enough to contact the ball; he can only do that by standing on one leg and swinging with the other. In other words, it's only real pressure when the player is a step away. Not three steps, like you might think under panic.

The yellow jersey moved in closer. I took my eyes off the field ahead and looked at him. A tall guy, with a dark crew cut. Three steps away.

Not real pressure. Not yet.

I moved diagonally up the field. A diagonal cut gives you much better vision than running straight ahead.

The yellow jersey moved to within two steps.

Almost real pressure. But I didn't panic. Instead, I slowed a fraction.

I took a last-minute look to see if passing was a better option. It wasn't. Their zone defense was still in place.

As the tall crew cut closed in, I did a half dribble, as if getting ready to pass long with the instep of my foot. I had already made a couple of bomb passes earlier in the game. It would look like I was about to try another.

From the soft half dribble, the ball was set up for a long kick. I drew my foot back.

The fake worked.

Crew Cut threw his body right to block the pass. In the split second while he was wrong-footed, and as my kicking foot came down, I pointed my toes downward. I cut the ball left, behind my supporting leg. The ball chipped sideways a couple of steps.

I was ready for the misdirection of the ball.

He wasn't.

I sprinted forward, leaving him a half step behind.

But I didn't relax. Too often, a defender will nip the ball from behind. Since he was chasing me from the right side, I used the outside of my left foot to dribble the ball ahead. As I ran, I made sure I kept my body between him and the ball.

I could see their zone defense begin to break down, just a little. The one player still behind me left them a man short to cover the rest of our guys.

If I could beat one more player . . .

Another yellow jersey drifted toward me. A short guy with wide shoulders. It left Steve open on the left for a pass. But if I dumped the ball off to him, their zone would close, and Steve would have nowhere to go.

Again, I thought it would be worth the risk to hold on to the ball.

Wide Shoulders cruised toward me. I pulled my right foot back as if I were going to give Steve the push pass at a 45-degree angle. Instead of passing it, though, I stepped over and to the left of the ball, spun my body clockwise, and cut the ball with the instep of my left foot. The ball popped to my right, catching Wide Shoulders on his wrong foot as he expected the pass on the left.

With just enough space and time, I burst ahead. Now there were two behind me.

Johnnie cut through the middle at full sprint and drew two yellow defenders. That left a gap up the middle.

I burst ahead with only thirty yards between me and the goalie. And four of our blue jerseys were moving into the open.

Johnnie stopped and ran to the side.

One yellow stayed with him. The other hesitated, and a third yellow player ran into him.

In the sudden confusion, I saw a chance to power forward. Now there were only two guys between me and the goalie.

I had ten steps of open space. Taking them all, I dribbled ahead at full speed.

I dipped my left shoulder, faked another pass, and

stepped into the ball with a full power instep kick to the right side of the net.

My fake pass didn't fool either of the last two defenders. Nor did it fool the goalie, who began to throw himself to the right corner of the goal.

Their sweeper had also guessed right. He jumped right to trap the ball. It hit him on the inside of his calf, which deflected the ball left.

It wasn't what I had planned.

But it wasn't what the goalie had planned, either.

Instead of an easy save on the right side of the net, he had to try to change direction. And he slipped, falling flat on his face.

On his stomach, he could only watch helplessly as the ball slowly rolled into the left side of the net.

It was my first goal of the tournament.

And it was enough to win the game.

Fifteen

Late that afternoon, I joined Leontine in front of her computer in her bedroom. The wall behind it held posters of Mickey Mouse, Bugs Bunny, and Big Bird. She had explained them to me once. Streaking her hair purple, orange, and green and dressing in black made her a rebel against boring people like me who wanted to look normal. The cartoon posters were a way for her to rebel against people who followed each other like sheep and raved over the "in" rock bands and movie stars. I'd rather use my energy for soccer and not worry about what was cool.

"Look at this," she said, pointing at her computer.

I pulled up a chair. With Bugs and Mickey staring down at me, I watched the screen as she clicked her mouse button. Colors and images flickered before us.

"I'm on-line," she said. "Hitting a website called belcher.com."

"Hang on," I said. "Back up. Belcher? Is it a website about burping?"

"No. It's someone's name. A person who lives in Roaring River. That's where the Riggins family came from. Remember?"

"I'm still lost."

"When I went surfing this afternoon, first thing I did was search for the local library. Most towns have libraries. Most public libraries offer Internet access."

"I get it," I said, waiting for the computer to download new images. "You chatted with the local librarian."

"No," she said. "I didn't have any luck. But I did have a brainstorm. If Roaring River was too small for a public library, I thought I might be able to hook up with a local elementary school. Lots of school libraries are on-line."

"So you patched into a local school?"

"It wasn't that easy," she said, enjoying the fact that I couldn't guess right. "I had to search for a North Carolina education directory. All I could find was an e-mail address."

As she talked, an image began to expand on the screen. It was a newspaper article with most of the headline cut off. In the center, a large black-and-white photo started to slowly paint across the screen. I listened to Leontine as I watched the photo grow line by line.

"So I fired off a message," she said. "Asking for someone to give me a time and location to meet in an on-line chat room to answer questions about the Riggins family. And I got lucky. The school principal happened to check her mailbox about an hour later."

"Yeah?" I said. The photo on the computer screen showed a family: a mom, a dad, and a boy, maybe two years old. It was one of those Sears portraits, with a fake background. Everyone was smiling. But the mom and dad did not look like a younger version of Mr. and Mrs. Riggins. And the boy had dark curly hair, nothing like Caleb's.

"Her name was Lola Max," Leontine said.

"The lady in this photo?"

"The school principal."

"Oh," I said. I began to scan the article. It was about a car accident.

"Anyway," Leontine said. "Mrs. Max e-mailed me back right away. She remembered the Riggins family very well and said my request for information about them was so unusual that she wanted to talk with me. She sent her telephone number and asked me to call. Dad gave me the okay, and I called her."

"Go on," I said. The article described how a cement truck with no brakes ran through a red light at the bottom of a hill.

"When I told her I was looking for some background information on them since they had moved to Lake Havasu City, she said she would fax me a newspaper article from their local newspaper."

"We don't have a fax machine," I said.

"Exactly, Einstein," she answered. "So Mrs. Max took the article over to a computer-genius friend of hers with a website. Someone named Sam Belcher."

"Belcher.com," I said, not looking up from my reading. The cement truck had hit a car in the intersection. The whole family—all of the people in the photo—had been in that car. All of them had died.

"Yes," Leontine answered. "Belcher.com. This Sam Belcher scanned the article and posted it on his website. And now, all I have to do is print it out."

Leontine clicked her mouse button a few more times. The print command came up on the screen, interrupting my reading.

"It sounds like a lot of complicated work," I said. "What's the big deal? Why was Mrs. Max in such a hurry to get this to you?"

"Didn't you read the article?" Leontine asked.

"I was just scanning through it," I said.

"The family in that article was the Riggins family," Leontine said.

"It was a terrible accident, so I don't want to say it's not a big deal. But what's the big deal that they had the same name?" I asked.

"Read the article closely," she said. "The mother and father are Louise and Charlie Riggins. The boy's name was Caleb."

"But still . . . ," I began.

"You don't get it."

"No," I said. I didn't get it. I was angry that I couldn't understand. "So enlighten me."

"Mrs. Max went to her school records," Leontine explained. "We compared birth certificates over the telephone. The one we have here in Lake Havasu for Caleb Riggins is identical to the one for the Caleb

Riggins who died in a car accident in Roaring River almost fourteen years ago."

"Identical," I said, wanting to be sure I heard right.

"Identical." Leontine went to the printer and picked up the copy of the newspaper article. She waved it at me.

"Several months after this family died in a car accident in North Carolina," she said, "another Riggins family showed up here in Arizona."

I shook my head, puzzled. "Are you saying Caleb Riggins isn't really Caleb Riggins?"

"I don't know what I'm saying," she said. "All I know is that this is getting weirder all the time."

Sixteen

Half an hour later, I was at the police station. I parked my mountain bike, locked it, and ran inside. A couple of policemen nodded hello to me. I nodded back but didn't stop to talk.

I found Mom at her usual place, behind a desk near the front. I knew what the rest of the station looked like from a tour she had arranged for me once. In the back were the holding cells, but other than that, it looked like any office.

"Win your game?" Mom asked with a smile. She faced a machine with a bunch of switches and wore a telephone headset.

"Yup," I said. "Two to one. But look at this."

I handed her the article that Leontine had printed. Mom read it within seconds, pushing hair out of her face as she leaned forward over it.

"Charlie Riggins," she read out loud. "A grocery store manager. His wife, Louise. And a son named Caleb. But the photo . . ."

"Doesn't look like the Riggins family we know," I said. "Mom, you're always looking for mysteries. Well, this one's real."

Mom stared off into space for a few moments. A strange look crossed her face. Then she snapped her fingers and flicked a switch on the dispatch machine.

"Captain Briscoe?" she said into the headset microphone. "It's Michelle. Would you mind coming here for a few moments?"

I couldn't hear his answer, of course, but right away the sound of hard heels on tile floor reached me. Captain Briscoe walked like a drill sergeant in the marines. He looked like one too. He had a gray crew cut, square face, thick neck, and broad shoulders.

"Hello, Matt," he said, shaking my hand. "What brings you here?"

Mom gave him the newspaper article. "Remember I brought you some concerns about the Riggins family? You might find this interesting."

"All right," he said after reading it. "I'll agree it's strange to find a family with the same names."

Mom took a deep breath. "Captain, you know I spend a lot of time trying to learn about detective work."

It might have been my imagination, but I thought I saw Captain Briscoe fight the twitch of a smile. "Yes," he said. "I do know that."

"I've learned that there's something people can do to change their identities," Mom said. "I'm sure you know about it. They look for people about the same age who have died. They send away for the dead person's birth certificate and use it to apply for a driver's license, credit cards . . . a new identity. No one ever cross-checks against death certificates."

"Yes," Captain Briscoe admitted. "I know of that happening. But this . . ."

"Is a whole family," Mom said. "If the father and mother and son were born about the same time as those killed in the accident, think of how easy it would be to give a whole family a new identity from the dead people's birth certificates. Especially if the family lived so far across the country from Roaring River that no one would recognize their names and connect them to the people who died in the car accident."

"How did you connect them?" Captain Briscoe asked.

I explained.

"I don't know," he said. "This is so far-fetched. And the Charlie Riggins we know is a respectable businessperson. There are probably thousands of Charlie Rigginses across the country."

"But how many with a wife named Louise and a son named Caleb?" Mom asked.

"Good point," he said. "But why would they go to this trouble?"

"I bet we could answer that if we knew who they were before they changed identities," Mom said. "Maybe Charlie was a drug dealer. Or a wanted murderer. Or—"

Mom's eyes were beginning to have that excited mystery shine.

"Hold on, hold on, hold on," Captain Briscoe said. "You have to be very careful about what you say. If you're wrong and rumors get started, Charlie Riggins could sue you for slander."

As he thought, Captain Briscoe rolled the article into a tube and tapped it with his right hand against the palm of his left hand.

"This is what I'll do," he said. "I'll photocopy this article. First thing tomorrow—when the records offices are open—I'll make some phone calls to look into this."

He shot a warning glance at Mom. "Remember, you keep this to yourself. Last thing I need is for the department to know that I'm actually involving myself in one of your crazy mysteries."

"Thank you, Captain," Mom said.

"But . . . ," I said.

They both looked at me.

"If Mr. Riggins is some kind of criminal," I said, "tomorrow might be too late. Caleb has been gone a day already."

"I don't think we need to worry," Captain Briscoe said after a few moments of thought. "At this point, Riggins doesn't know we're checking into his background. Say this does turn out to be something. Nothing will go wrong as long as Charlie Riggins thinks he is safe."

He directed his frown at me. "Which means you can now leave this in police hands."

He cleared his throat. "Right, Matt?"

"Um, yes, sir," I said. "Absolutely right."

As if I'd ever do anything crazy like my mom.

Seventeen

In the darkness, a *Tyrannosaurus rex* roared as it charged toward me. I hardly noticed. I'd sat there for half of the movie that night, and I couldn't even remember eating my popcorn.

Who were Charlie, Louise, and Caleb Riggins? Why had they moved to Lake Havasu City? Were they running from something? Where had they gone?

The *T. rex* pushed a van off a cliff. Steve, beside me in the theater, slurped on his cola as he leaned forward, totally focused on the movie.

But I couldn't get Caleb's note out of my mind. Over and over, questions kept repeating themselves. Where were Caleb and his parents? Why had they disappeared? I realized that without Caleb, our team might not make it to the nationally televised finals—

"Hey!" I said out loud. People in front of me turned around to glare.

"Sorry," I whispered to them. I didn't explain that I had just been hit by a lightning bolt of a thought.

The nationally televised finals. Caleb was our star scorer. If we went to the tournament, Caleb would be seen on televisions all across the country. If Charlie Riggins and his wife and son were in hiding under a new identity, of course Charlie would do everything possible to keep Caleb off television.

I pulled together the threads that were dangling in my mind. Caleb had only been three years old when the Riggins family moved to Lake Havasu City. Nobody remembered much about anything before they were three. Caleb wouldn't know anything about the identity change.

I remembered that Dad had told me about Caleb writing a story in first grade about a twin brother. What if it were true? That would explain why Charlie Riggins had gotten so mad.

Wow. Wow. Wow.

And what else had Dad said? Something about a golden bridge. Could that be a real place?

A golden bridge! Maybe there was a way to find out who Caleb had been.

"Steve," I whispered, "I'll be right back."

He didn't even hear me. He was watching the dinosaurs search for more food. He didn't know about the newspaper article and the car accident. Mom had asked me to keep that information to myself.

I ran up the aisle. I got to a pay phone. I called Leontine at home. I told her what I was thinking and asked her to do me a favor by searching for more stuff on the Internet. She told me she'd have it ready by the time I got home after the movie. I thanked her and hung up.

Maybe popcorn is brain food. Because as I walked back into the darkness of the movie and saw the dinosaurs trying to chomp more people, I had another thought.

The dogs. Who was feeding the dogs?

Caleb's note had said they were leaving for a while. Long enough so that Caleb would miss the entire tournament?

Who was feeding the dogs while they were gone?

A neighbor? It would have to be a brave neighbor because those dogs were running loose. If it wasn't a neighbor, maybe it was . . . As I sat down in my theater seat, I groaned at how obvious it was.

They had taken the pontoon boat from the driveway. If Charlie Riggins wanted to keep Caleb out of town, spending the week on Lake Havasu made sense. It would look like a family spring-break vacation and keep Caleb from sneaking to any more soccer games.

Which meant Charlie Riggins could also stay close enough to home to feed the dogs.

I grabbed Steve's elbow.

"Come on," I whispered. "We're getting out of here."

"What! The movie's not finished."

"Trust me," I insisted. I had a copy of the article in my back pocket. "I'll explain while you're driving us back to Caleb's house."

Eighteen

Two hours later, we were still sitting in Steve's mom's minivan. We had parked in the shadows between street-lights, a half block down from the Riggins house. The front of the van faced McCullough Avenue, giving us plenty of time to notice if any cars or trucks turned onto the street where we waited. Steve had slouched down as far as possible behind the steering wheel. I was slouched on the passenger side.

"I thought being a detective was more cool than this," he said. "You know. Beautiful women who need help. Chasing bad guys. Stuff like that."

"I agree," I said. "Detectives should drive Corvettes or Porsches, not family vans with jelly beans on the floor and old, dog-hair-covered blankets in the back-seat."

Steve pointed at the newspaper article on the console between our seats. "If it wasn't for that, I'd think we were crazy."

"We'll give it a half hour more, okay?" I turned my wrist so my watch could catch some light. "I need to get home by then anyway."

Steve snorted. "And detectives definitely don't have to get home on time."

"Yeah, yeah, yeah," I said.

"What about when we leave?" Steve asked. "I still think we should get some police here."

"No," I said. "They'll probably think that this is a dumb idea."

"My point exactly. And we missed the best half of the mov—"

He snapped his mouth shut and slumped lower behind the steering wheel.

Headlights.

I ducked lower, too.

The light swept over us as the car turned into the street. The car passed us. I saw it wasn't a car. But a Blazer.

Charlie Riggins.

We watched by turning and peeking over the seats through the back window.

When the Blazer pulled into the driveway, the dogs came running around the corner from the back. Mr. Riggins climbed out and squatted next to the animals. He rubbed their heads and their bellies.

Of all the stuff I knew already, that one little action made me the maddest. How could he be such a jerk to his family but still love his dogs so much?

A few moments later, Charlie Riggins walked around to the back of the house. Both dogs followed.

"Too bad we're parked so far away," Steve whispered. "Your idea about the tape was a good one."

On our way here from the movie theater, we had decided we would follow him as far as we could. Then we would turn around and tell the police where he had gone. I had suggested trying to put some duct tape over one of his taillights. With only one taillight showing, it would be much easier to follow him from a distance.

"I know," I said. "But if he catches us . . ."

After talking it over, we had decided there was so little traffic at this time of night we could stay a long ways back and follow without losing him.

Which—five minutes later—we did.

Nineteen

Charlie Riggins backed out of his driveway. The headlights of his Blazer shone through the inside of the minivan. Steve and I were ready, though, and had ducked beneath the dash. To Charlie Riggins, the minivan would seem empty.

He sped by. His taillights glowed red as he braked for the corner. He turned right. Down McCullough Avenue toward the lake.

"Like you," I said.

"What?" Steve asked. "You *like* me?"

"No. The taillights. They should be easy to follow. Just remember they're like you."

"Like *me?*"

I grinned. "Yeah. Tall and skinny."

"Ha, ha," Steve said. "You want to follow him on your mountain bike?"

Steve waited a few seconds after Riggins had turned before starting the minivan. He put it into gear and we pulled ahead slowly. When we reached the corner, those tall and skinny taillights showed the Blazer had at least a two-block lead. Close enough that we could stay with him. Far enough away that he probably wouldn't notice us.

We got even luckier. At the stop sign, we had to wait for a car on our left to pass us. That put a car between us and Riggins all the way down McCullough Avenue.

"What do you think?" Steve asked as we neared the business section of town at the bottom of the long hill. "Is he going to the marina?"

"I doubt it," I answered. "That would mean the pontoon boat is docked there. It would be too easy for Caleb to escape."

Sure enough, Riggins turned left to reach Highway 95 instead of continuing straight to go over the London Bridge to the marina.

"Good," I said.

"Good? What if he's leaving town?"

"Exactly," I said. "The lake only goes as far as the dam at Parker. And that's barely twenty miles away. I doubt he put his pontoon boat in the river on the other side of the dam. That means he's got to pull off between here and the dam. At the most, we'll only have to follow him twenty minutes before turning around to get the police."

We kept following. Riggins stuck to the speed limit through town. And he stuck to the raised speed limit outside of town. He probably didn't want to risk calling attention to himself by getting a speeding ticket.

That made it easy for us to follow him. We gave him a half-mile lead. Even though the desert highway was empty of all vehicles except for his and ours, I wasn't worried. To him, we were just another pair of headlights.

The moon had risen over the mountain ridges, almost bright enough for us to drive without head-lights. It gave a beautiful blue-gray glow to the barren desert, so strong that crosslike shadows fell from every cactus we passed.

The highway south of Lake Havasu City is mainly straight and flat for about ten miles, with the lake on the right just out of sight. As the highway nears the end of the valley, it begins to dip and twist and turn where the low mountains on each side grow closer together.

All the way along the straight sections of highway, those tall and skinny taillights drew us like red bea-cons. We lost the lights briefly as the highway cut into the first dipping turn. Thirty seconds later, they reappeared as we made the turn, then disappeared again as Riggins topped the small hill ahead of us and dropped down the other side.

No other cars had joined us. We were still the only vehicles on this stretch of highway. It was dark and lonely, with the ribbon of pavement gleaming pale beneath the moonlight.

"Man," Steve said. "You know what this area is like. There are a couple of cutoff roads that lead from the highway to the lake. If he turns off while he's out of sight, we'll pass him without even knowing it."

"Maybe speed up?" I offered.

Steve gave the minivan a little more gas as we went up the hill.

As we crested the hill, Steve slammed on the brakes.

We didn't have to worry about losing Riggins. The Blazer was just ahead, parked on the shoulder, with the emergency flashers on.

"Now what!" Steve said. "We can't stop. But if we keep going, we might lose him."

We had less than twenty seconds to decide.

"Slow down," I said, "just like you would if you were passing any other car. When we get past him, we'll pull over and hide somewhere off the highway and wait for him to pass us again."

Ten seconds.

"You don't think he knows we're following him?"

"Impossible," I answered. "We're just another set of headlights."

Five seconds. Charlie Riggins suddenly stepped onto the highway with a flashlight, waving his arms to stop us.

Steve slammed on the brakes. "Now what?"

I didn't answer. I was too busy diving into the backseat. Unlike Steve, I was wearing our soccer team sweats. Mr. Riggins might not recognize me, but he'd know the team uniform.

"Now what?" Steve repeated.

"Stop," I said, getting down on the floor and pulling a smelly blanket over me. "Like you would for any guy waving you down. Tell him you're on your way to

Parker, and you'll get help for him there. What's he going to do, pull a gun?"

Steve stopped. He rolled down the window.

"Car problems," Charlie Riggins said. From a crack under the blanket, I watched Mr. Riggins shine the flashlight into Steve's face. "Thanks for stopping."

"I'm going to Parker," Steve said. "I'll send a tow truck back to help."

I tried not to sneeze from the dog hairs on the smelly blanket. Toys on the floor of the van pushed uncomfortably into my stomach and legs.

"No, you won't," Riggins told Steve with a sudden snarl. "I've seen you before. You're going to tell me why you followed me from my house."

"But—"

"Don't but me, punk. Your left headlight is burned out. I first noticed you when you pulled out of my street. I want you to tell me why you're following me."

That made me wrong about us being just another set of headlights.

"But—"

"Are you the jerk who messed with my dogs last night?" As Charlie Riggins spoke, he played his flashlight beam over the inside of the van. I didn't know it until later, but he stopped the beam on the newspaper article that I had left on the console in plain sight. The picture of the dead family must have leaped out at him.

"Get this van on the shoulder now," Mr. Riggins nearly yelled. He pulled a pistol from his jacket. "Or I'll shoot you where you sit."

The gun, of course, made me wrong again.

Twenty

Charlie Riggins stayed beside the driver's window as Steve slowly drove to the shoulder of the highway. He didn't give Steve a chance to hit the gas and escape. He didn't give me a chance to talk to Steve.

Steve put the minivan in park and turned on the flashers so no one would hit the van.

"Out," Mr. Riggins barked.

"Wh . . . wh . . . where are we going?" Steve asked.

"You'll find out soon enough. Just like soon enough you're going to tell me where you got that article."

Steve opened the door slowly. The interior light of the minivan flashed on. I held my breath and stayed under the blanket, shivering with fear. Why hadn't I listened to Captain Briscoe and stayed out of this?

Charlie Riggins didn't notice me on the floor in the back.

"You made a big mistake, kid," I heard him say as Steve stepped out. "If people here know about that car accident, I have nothing to lose. Which means you better not try anything stupid."

Because the driver's window was still open, I heard them both walk to the truck. Once they were inside, I heard the Blazer drive away.

I pushed up quickly, throwing the blanket off and gulping for breath.

What could I do? If I followed, the burned-out headlight would give me away. If I turned around and went for the police, we might never find them. And even if we did, it might be too late for Steve, or Caleb.

I watched those tall and skinny taillights get smaller in the darkness. Suddenly, they brightened as Charlie Riggins hit the brakes.

Was he stopping to turn around? I got ready to dive under the smelly blanket again.

No! He was turning off the highway, toward the lake.

That helped my decision. But not much. Going back to Lake Havasu City for help—or even going the shorter distance ahead to the stores and restaurants near Parker Dam and calling back to Lake Havasu City—might take too long. Risky as it sounded, it seemed like all I could do was follow the truck on foot.

I began to open the door. Then I remembered the interior light and froze. If Charlie Riggins saw it flash on, he might turn back.

I waited for the truck's taillights to disappear as the Blazer drove alongside a gully that led to the lake shore.

I finally opened the door and hopped out.

I took two steps. Then I thought of something.

I turned back to the minivan. First I ran to the rear and dug around to find a tire iron. It was all I could think of for protection. Then I rummaged in the glove compartment and found a pen and paper. It took less than a minute for me to do what I needed to do.

When I was ready, I jumped out of the van.

Tire iron in hand, I hit the ground running.

It was easy to follow the sandy road that led to the lake. Moonlight gave me a clear view of the desert brush on each side. Where the road dropped into the gully, I dipped in and out of dark shadows as I ran.

It only took ten minutes to near the lake's edge. I saw the Blazer parked at the end of the road. I expected the pontoon boat to be anchored nearby.

I was wrong again.

The ten minutes it had taken for me to get there had been enough time. Charlie Riggins had tied a sweatshirt around Steve's face so he would be too blind to try to escape. Steve sat in the front of a small rubber dinghy, the one from the pontoon boat. And they were already motoring away from shore.

The ripples looked like silver snakes on the calm dark water. I hid behind the Blazer and watched as they moved farther away. The pontoon boat, then, was somewhere on the other side.

There is something about sound on water. People who fish will tell you that in their own boat, they can barely hear each other above the noise of their outboard motor. So they talk louder. But for some reason, their conversation carries away from the boat above the sound of the outboard, so people a couple hundred yards away can easily hear what they're saying.

I heard.

"Just so you know, punk, you're going to spend some time with Caleb. About as long as it takes to sink a pontoon boat."

Twenty-One

You're going to spend some time with Caleb. About as long as it takes to sink a pontoon boat.

Did that mean what I thought it meant? Was Charlie Riggins going to drown Steve and Caleb?

Panic squeezed me. What could I do? What could I do? What could—

I put my right thumb in my mouth and bit as hard as I could. The pain was like a slap across the face. I took a deep breath and remembered Dad telling me how wonderful prayer was. Not only could I ask God for help, but it was also a calming reminder of God's presence in everything. I prayed. It did help me. Then I tried to think rationally and decided to rely on what I knew.

I told myself I needed to imagine this was a soccer play. I'm the last man back with the ball. Just my goalie is behind me. Twenty guys are spread out on the field in front of me—nine on my team, eleven on the other. I see two guys coming at me to take the ball.

Look at the situation. Make the best choice possible in the time remaining. And act on your decision.

All right, I thought. I would give myself however long it took to come up with the best solution. Fortunately, I had more than the one or two seconds I normally have on the soccer field.

Looking at it that way relaxed me.

The situation was simple. Once Charlie Riggins reached the pontoon boat, he was going to find a way to sink it. I needed to be there. Without getting caught.

Did I have a boat of my own?

No.

What did I have?

A tire iron. And the Blazer parked beside me.

Could I use the Blazer?

No. It wouldn't float

What else did I have?

I knew how to swim.

I gave myself another half minute to try to find any other solution. I couldn't.

It wasn't even a mile across the lake here. I had never swum from shore to shore, but I knew I could do it. I was in good shape from soccer, and I'd had plenty of swimming lessons. The water wasn't so cold that it would kill me. I didn't have to worry about sharks.

And there definitely wasn't time to go for help. Swimming was my only choice.

I just had to get in the water.

I dropped the tire iron and leaned against the Blazer as I kicked off my shoes and peeled off my sweat suit and T-shirt. It left me barefoot in my shorts.

Briefly, I wondered about the tire iron. I told myself it was too heavy to carry as I swam.

Then I noticed the locked fuel flap on the side of the truck. It gave me an idea. I could at least use the tire iron to pry it open, couldn't I?

And once it was open, I could . . .

I grinned in the darkness. Whatever happened in the next half hour, I would be happy knowing I had done something to make trouble for Charlie Riggins.

Once I was finished with the gas tank, I hid my clothes. If Charlie Riggins got back without seeing me in the lake, I didn't want him to know I'd been here.

Then I stepped into the lake. I walked until the water was waist deep. The water sent shock waves running up my body. I didn't stop to think about how cold it was. I dove forward into the dark water.

Twenty-Two

The putt-putt of the small outboard motor on the rubber dinghy got farther and farther away. Riggins was cutting at an angle across the lake. By the time I started swimming, it was at least the length of four soccer fields away from shore. As I swam, that distance grew and grew.

I wasn't worried about Riggins seeing or hearing me in the water behind him.

While the moonlight showed the jagged edges of the low mountains on the other side of the lake and the pale gleam of my arms as I lifted them out of the water, most of my body was hidden in the depths of the dark water. Even if he happened to look back, he would probably see nothing but lake.

I tried to swim steady. I tried to block all thoughts from my mind. I tried not to remember that Lake Havasu was really a dammed-up section of the Colorado River, and that somewhere far below me was the old riverbed. And that the water was probably hundreds of cold, dark feet deep, and . . .

Soccer. Soccer. Soccer. I put my mind on soccer.

The Mavericks had won three games, tied one, and lost one. We shared second place with two other teams. If we ended in a tie with any team, the higher ranking would go to the team with the most goals scored. That meant we really, really needed Caleb. Tomorrow morning, if we all got to the . . .

I gritted my teeth and kept swimming.

Tomorrow morning, *when* we all got to the soccer field, we would keep feeding the ball to Caleb and let him pour in the goals. That would leave us with one last game in the afternoon. If we won that, we would move on to the sudden-death play-off on Thursday.

I pictured players on the field—Johnnie Rivers cutting across for a long pass, Stew Schmid diving with his arms stretched to stop a goal, me breaking up the field and beating defenders.

The soccer thoughts calmed me.

I got into a rhythm as I swam. My breathing grew harder, but I had plenty of energy. My eyes got used to the water. And no big fish came up to drag me down.

Before I realized it, I was halfway across the lake.

I stopped and treaded water. The stars put on an incredible show above me. The lights of Lake Havasu City glowed fifteen miles down the valley.

I looked ahead to the far shore for any sign of the pontoon boat. I saw nothing. I listened hard and heard the putt-putt of the outboard motor straight ahead.

I began to swim again. Two-thirds of the way across the lake, I began counting my strokes.

Two hundred and one. Two hundred and two. Two hundred and three.

Two hundred and four. Two hundred and five. Two hundred and—

The putt-putt sound of the motor suddenly sounded louder!

I stopped and treaded water again. I pushed my wet hair back and strained to look ahead.

I realized this putt-putt sounded deeper than the outboard motor on the rubber dinghy.

Then I saw it. Like a shadow pulling loose from the dark outline of the far shore. It was the Rigginses' pontoon boat. Heading toward me. About the length of five soccer fields away.

Where were they going?

I watched a moment, and the answer came to me.

It would be much smarter to sink the pontoon boat in the center of the lake. In the bottom of the old river canyon now filled by this lake, it would never be found.

As I waited, the pontoon boat grew more clear in the moonlight. It would reach me in a couple of minutes. It would reach the center of the lake in a couple more minutes.

Would Charlie Riggins see my head sticking out of the water as the pontoon boat passed by?

I couldn't take the chance. I swam out of its path. Then I did the dead man's float, hoping I wouldn't *become* a dead man.

As the pontoon boat neared, I glanced up and saw that Charlie Riggins was at the wheel. He had tied the rubber dinghy behind with a rope. I guessed that when the pontoon boat began to sink, he would make his getaway in the dinghy.

What, I wondered, *would stop Caleb and Steve from jumping off the pontoon boat and swimming away as it sank?*

I tried to put myself in Charlie Riggins's place. What would I do? I didn't like the answer. I would tie Caleb and Steve to the pontoon boat.

I knew I was right. During the time I was swimming across the lake, Riggins had plenty of time to get to the far shore with his outboard motor. But he hadn't moved the pontoon boat right away—which meant he must have taken some time to tie up Steve and Caleb. Only then would he have started the boat's engine.

I watched the pontoon boat pass me. I wished I were close enough to swim hard and catch up to the rubber dinghy that was being towed behind it. That way I could hitch a ride without anyone seeing me.

Instead, I had to chase the boat.

I didn't know how much farther Riggins planned to take the pontoon boat. I didn't know how he was going to sink it. I didn't know how long it would take to sink.

I just knew I had to get there before it went under.

Twenty-Three

I used the breaststroke as I followed. It was slower than an overhand crawl, but it let me keep my head above water so I could watch the pontoon boat.

The good news was that I had guessed right. Once Charlie Riggins reached the middle of the lake, he cut the motor.

The bad news also was that I had guessed right. The middle of the lake was still a long swim away.

I pushed as hard as I could, staying with the breaststroke and frog kicks. If I went to a flutter kick for more speed, I would splash, and the lake was very quiet without the sound of the outboard motor. I could not afford to let Charlie Riggins know I was nearby. It would be too easy for him to chase me down with the rubber dinghy.

Across that silence, I heard a big whack of steel against something solid. And another. And another.

I could not make sense of it.

The whacking continued, ringing clear over the water.

I pusher harder and began to gasp for air. I'd been swimming for at least half an hour. If it hadn't been for endless soccer practices and endless soccer games, I would have had to turn back to shore a long time ago.

Whack! Whack! Whack! Whack!

Then silence.

Was it my imagination, or did I see two dark figures move toward the back of the pontoon boat?

I saw them only briefly before they both crouched out of sight.

Then I heard the sound of the rubber dinghy's outboard engine. The two people must have jumped into it.

Seconds later, I saw the low outline of the rubber dinghy as it left the pontoon boat and headed for the shore.

And seconds after that, I saw the pontoon boat tilt forward and begin to sink!

With the outboard motor now making lots of noise, I didn't have to worry about splashing.

I switched back to an overhand crawl with a flutter kick. And I gave it everything I could.

The pontoon boat was sinking, and I was still at least a soccer field away!

My lungs began to heave. My legs and arms began to hurt. But I had to keep pushing.

I stopped for a second and lifted my head out of the water.

The rubber dinghy was out of sight. In place of its

motor, I heard my friends screaming for help. The pontoon boat had begun to go under!

I slammed my face back into the lake and propelled myself forward. *Harder. Harder. Harder.*

Half a soccer field away. A third of the pontoon boat already under.

My throat was raw from sucking in air. The only thing keeping my arms and legs in motion was terror. *Harder. Harder. Harder.*

Somehow, I reached the pontoon boat. It was half-way under and sliding down fast.

I grabbed a rail and pulled myself up.

"Matt!" Steve yelled. He was on the rear deck of the pontoon boat. The front half—the cabin part—was already underwater.

"Matt!"

I could only suck in air. No way could I talk.

"We're tied to the rail," Steve said. "You've got to get us loose."

I held the rail and staggered up the deck toward Steve. His arms were tied to the upper railing. His legs to the lower railing. Caleb was tied to the railing a few feet away.

The water was almost at their feet!

I heaved and tried to catch my breath, still unable to talk. I found the knots around Steve's feet. If I didn't do his feet first, they'd be underwater even before his hands were loose.

My cold, wet fingers fumbled with the knots. The knots were too tight. I couldn't pull the rope loose.

"Can't do it," I gasped. I stood, staggering again as the pontoon boat tilted more. "I can't get the rope undone!"

And the water reached his feet.

Twenty-Four

The moonlight showed a couple of life jackets floating nearby. Life jackets that would not help as the pontoon boat dragged Steve and Caleb under.

"Ax!" Caleb cried. "Get the ax!"

"What?" I asked. I had to grab the railing beside Steve to keep my balance. In the dark between me and Caleb, I could not see his face.

"He used an ax to punch holes in the pontoons. Get the ax."

That explained the whacking sound.

"Where is it?"

"He left it on the deck. Maybe it slid down toward the cabin." *The cabin that was already underwater!*

Without thinking about how scared I was, I dove. It was like diving into cold midnight. My ears roared as the water closed over my head.

I kicked downward, blindly reaching with my hands. My clawing fingers raked the outside wall of

102

the cabin. I followed the wall down to where it met the deck. If the ax was still on board, that's where I would find it.

Just as I was about to run out of air, I felt the smooth long handle of the ax. I grabbed it and pushed upward.

I reached the surface. I had to hold on to the railing with my free hand to get my balance on the tilted deck. The pontoon boat was almost at the angle of a set of stairs.

Then I realized the worst of it.

Steve's feet were underwater. How was I going to cut the knots loose? Getting his hands free wouldn't help if his legs were still tied to the pontoon boat. And at best, there was only a minute left.

I felt panic squeezing me again, like a giant snake closing in for the kill.

Soccer, I told myself, *soccer. Sudden-death overtime. I'm the last man back with the ball. Attackers moving in. What would I do?*

Look at the situation. Make the best choice possible in the time remaining. And act on the decision.

I lifted the ax above my head.

"Matt!" Steve yelled. "What are you do—"

I slammed the ax down.

Not at Steve's wrists. Not at the rope around the railing. But at the railing itself, a couple of feet away from Steve.

The aluminum pipe of the railing sheared in half.

I took another mighty swing and cut through the lower railing.

Then I staggered past the motor to Caleb.

With two more jumbo swings, I cut through the upper railing and then the lower railing.

I dropped the ax. It splashed to the deck at my feet and slid back toward the cabin.

I kicked at the lower rail, bending it away from me. I leaned into the upper rail, bending it too.

I grabbed Caleb and pulled him toward the breaks.

"Slide your hands toward me," I said. "Hurry!"

When his wrists reached the gap in the railing, his hands popped loose. Still knotted together, but no longer tied to the pontoon boat.

"You too," I called across to Steve. "Slide your hands loose. I'll be right there to help you with your legs."

Then I bent in the water. It was already up to Caleb's knees. I helped him slide his legs off the broken railing.

"Can't swim," he said. "Not with my hands and legs tied."

He probably didn't see my grin in the darkness. I already knew how to solve that problem. The floating life jackets had begun to bang against my legs.

I snatched one and shoved it into Caleb's chest. "Hold this down with your arms," I said. "I'll be right back."

I took another life jacket and sloshed over to Steve. He had already worked his hands loose.

"Take this!" I said.

He hugged it against himself.

I helped him slip his legs free from the lower railing.

Any later, and he would have been gone.

Without even a splash, the pontoon boat dropped out from under us just as we kicked away from the railing.

The three of us bobbed in the water. My friends were still tied but holding on to their life jackets. I stared at them, almost in a daze.

With some splashing, we joined together. Steve floated on a life jacket on my left, and Caleb floated on my right. I put an arm around each of them. I felt so tired, I might have gone under without their help.

I slowly kicked through the water, pointing us toward shore.

I imagined the pontoon boat behind us, drifting downward farther and farther in the midnight black of the water, until it settled somewhere on the ancient banks of the river, far, far below.

I didn't realize I was crying until I tasted the salt of my tears.

Twenty-Five

It was Tuesday afternoon. To warm up, our team—including Caleb Riggins—passed balls around on our half of the field.

In our morning game, Caleb had scored three goals to help the Mavericks win 4–1. If we won this final game and scored at least three goals, we were guaranteed a spot in the sudden-death finals. And that final game would probably be against the team we had beaten this morning. As I saw it, if we won with enough goals this afternoon, we'd have a good chance at winning the entire tournament to go on to the nationals.

I kicked the ball to Caleb. He made a move on Johnnie, drawing the ball back with his left foot, hitting it with the inside of his heel, popping it through Johnnie's legs, and picking it up on the other side.

Johnnie laughed and Caleb turned around to grin at me.

Already, last night's events hardly seemed real.

It had taken half an hour for Steve and Caleb and me to get close to shore. We were still a hundred yards away when two police cars roared down the road to the edge of the lake. Their flashing lights bounced eerie red-and-blue shadows off the desert brush as we shouted across the water to them.

I had not been surprised to see the state troopers. Just before leaving the minivan, I had written a note and stuck it beneath the driver's side windshield wiper. I hoped someone would notice the emergency flashers Steve had left on, stop, and read the note. It was a simple note, asking whoever found it to call the police and send them down the road to the lake.

The state troopers, of course, had arrived too late to catch Charlie and Louise Riggins. The Blazer was long gone, leaving behind a rubber dinghy and tire tracks in the sand as proof of their escape.

But today both Charlie and his wife were in jail in Lake Havasu City.

Desert highways, you see, are long and lonely with little traffic. The Rigginses had only traveled about ten miles before the truck came to a sputtering stop. My little trick before stepping into the water had been to add sand to the gas tank, and it had worked really well. We told the state troopers what had happened and they went out looking. They found the Rigginses standing beside the truck beneath the night stars, trying to hitch a ride.

Neither Charlie nor Louise, however, had given any

explanation for their crazy actions. They had hired a lawyer and refused to talk to anyone but him. All the police knew for sure was that Charlie and Louise and Caleb were not who they said they were—the police had confirmed that the Rigginses had taken on the identities of the dead family before moving to Lake Havasu City.

The police didn't know why. Nor did they know Caleb's real name or his background.

As for Caleb, he was almost relieved to have escaped his parents. During that long swim to shore from the sunken pontoon boat, Caleb had told me and Steve that Charlie and Louise had always treated him overly strictly, making him a near prisoner in their home all his life. If it hadn't been for soccer—his only escape—his life would have been totally miserable.

Arrangements had already been made with a school psychologist to help Caleb through the next few weeks, which would be difficult. After all, his parents had tried to drown him, and he had no idea why.

Me? I felt some freedom too. Freedom from caring about something as unimportant as appearances. Sure, my dad had shaved his head and ran a class-room zoo while Charlie Riggins wore three-piece suits and owned a beautiful house. Sure, people who didn't understand my parents joked about them. But Mom and Dad gave me love and care. That's what mattered. I was who I was because of how they had raised me. And I was going to be proud of it.

From the soccer field, I turned to wave at Mom, Dad, and Leontine. They were sitting in the stands, ready to scream and cheer and shout and make fools of themselves. They waved back. Dad, of course, waved carefully. He hadn't learned his lesson with Larry and had the snake draped around his shoulders. And there was a lot of room in the bleachers on both sides of my family because of it.

The referee blew his whistle to get the game started.

There was one minute left in the game. We were up 2–1, but we needed a third goal to qualify for the finals.

We pressed hard near their goal. Caleb and Steve passed the ball back and forth. Caleb got the ball from Steve and saw Johnnie open. Caleb kicked the ball hard, but his pass bounced off their defender and out the end zone.

Corner kick.

Forty-five seconds left.

We lined up quickly.

The Redland High Robins—wearing brown uniforms—formed a wall of defense in front of their net.

Steve took the kick from the corner.

He lofted the ball high. As it came down, one of their strikers broke away to punt the ball toward center field. Johnnie fought him for it, and the striker's kick wobbled the ball weakly toward me.

I trapped it and looked up. Two brown uniforms were dashing toward me.

Look at the situation. Make the best choice possible in the time remaining. And act on the decision.

Compared to a life or death situation, this didn't seem like pressure at all.

Caleb was hanging to the left side of the net, in the middle of all the remaining players. All I needed to do was get the ball to him. . . .

I faked a pass to my right, enough to get both attackers leaning that direction. Then, with a flick of my foot, I chipped the ball toward the left goal post.

It hung against the sky briefly. As it dropped, Caleb darted out from the pack of defenders—and timed his jump perfectly. He slammed his head forward, catching the ball flush in the center of his forehead.

The goalie didn't have a chance. The ball caught the underside of the crossbar and dropped in behind the goalie's shoulder.

Goal! Three to one! We were in the finals!

On the field we danced around, hugging and screaming.

Cheers and whistles and screams reached us from the stands.

The ref blew his whistle to end the game.

And everyone mobbed Caleb to congratulate him.

He had scored an important goal, all right. But it wasn't nearly as important as what happened when he walked off the field.

Caleb Riggins found himself staring at a kid identical to himself in every way.

Twenty-Six

I felt as shocked as Caleb looked.

People from the stands gathered around, as much to congratulate our team as to see what was happening. That's when I noticed Mom and Leontine off to the right, watching with big grins on their faces. And behind them was a Lake Havasu City police car, with Captain Briscoe leaning against it and grinning, too.

I pushed through the mob and marched straight toward them.

"Okay," I said to Mom and Leontine, "what's going on?"

"Can't you figure it out?" Mom answered. "After all, you're the one who pointed Leontine in the right direction last night."

"Last night . . . last night . . ." So many things had happened in such a short period of time, I felt dazed.

"When you called me from the movie theater,"

Leontine said. "Remember? The golden bridge? Internet search?"

All I had done was tell Leontine that maybe Caleb's first-grade story had been true, that maybe the golden bridge of Caleb's best memory as a three-year-old was a real place. Like the Golden Gate Bridge of San Francisco. And if the story was real and the place was real, maybe an Internet search for information on a little boy who had disappeared about thirteen years ago from that area might give us a clue.

Slowly, I began to understand. "Don't tell me," I said. "The twin brother from his story was true, too?"

"His name is Robert Masters," Mom said. "And he took an early flight to get here so Captain Briscoe could bring him down in time to watch some of the game. We wanted to keep it out of the media. Captain Briscoe said it would give the police a chance to complete the investigation in San Francisco and make an arrest there."

I turned back for another look at Caleb and the other guy. Twin brothers. Cool.

They had begun to walk away from the crowd, just the two of them. They would have a lot to talk about.

Me, too. I looked back at Mom. The detective gleam was in her eyes.

"Tell me everything," I said. "Arrests in San Francisco?"

She told me that Caleb Riggins was born in San Francisco as Thomas Masters with a twin named Robert. Their parents were very rich. A year later, their father died of a heart attack. Their mother remarried when the twins were two years old. A year later, Thomas drowned in an accident at the ocean. The tide pulled his body out to sea. Because of estate tax planning and inheritance laws, the life insurance policy on little Thomas Masters had been set up to pay millions. This was in a newspaper article that Leontine had found during her Internet search.

To the world, then, a child had drowned and his body had never been recovered. The real story was very different.

The twins' new stepfather, a man named Sydney Gilbert, had set up the drowning accident to collect on the life insurance. But he didn't actually go through with killing little Thomas. He figured if he ever got caught, he'd rather face time in jail for fraud than the electric chair for murder. So Sydney Gilbert had cut a deal with his brother and his brother's wife.

He gave them a lot of money to start a new life with Thomas, safely hidden in Lake Havasu City under a new name: Riggins. Charlie Riggins used his money well and became a successful businessman in the small town. To get their new name of Riggins, they'd done exactly as Mom had guessed. They'd researched newspapers across the country to find a family similar to theirs who had died. With copies of that family's birth certificates, they got new driver's licenses and new credit cards. Credit checks just showed an odd gap in activity—between the real Rigginses' deaths and the new Rigginses' use of their identities.

It was almost perfect. Thomas, of course, had not been old enough to really remember anything about his family. And Charlie and Louise Riggins got paid a lot of money to essentially baby-sit Thomas until he was old enough to go to college.

Their secret would never have been found out, if not for the upcoming televised soccer tournament. They were afraid that if Caleb went on national television, someone in San Francisco would see him and notice he looked identical to Robert Masters. Then, of course, all the questions would start. So they had done their best to keep him from playing in the tournament, knowing that the team had little chance without him. The stress of possibly being found out after all these years had driven Charlie Riggins to actually begin hitting Caleb. The thought made me wince. I listened and listened and listened.

"Wow . . . ," I said when Mom finished. "Caleb—I mean, Thomas—has another mother waiting for him in San Francisco."

"No," Mom said, "she's over there." Mom pointed at a grinning woman who looked a lot like Caleb. She had just stood back for a few minutes while her sons met. As we watched, she started toward them.

"What about the stepfather?" I asked.

"A real rat," Mom said. "He left the family a couple of years after Thomas disappeared. Fortunately, the twins' mom knew where to find him. He's probably under arrest by now. It will take a while to sort this all out. Captain Briscoe promised to keep me informed of everything."

"Like you're a real detective," I said, laughing. "Congratulations."

Mom grinned. I was proud of her. And proud to be part of the Carr family.

I nearly told her that, but I didn't have a chance.

Screams began in the middle of the crowd behind us. Screams of panic.

Above it all, I heard my dad's voice, shouting.

"Larry? Where are you?"

The three of us behind the fence leaned against it, so that it bent inward a bit without weight. I had my fingers wrapped around the linked steel.

We were on the safe side of the fence. Joey Saylor, the new kid, was inside, where he wasn't supposed to be. He was about the length of a football field away from us, on the walkway above a smelly duck pond. He had ragged blond hair that almost reached his shoulders. He wore black jeans, a black T-shirt, and new Nikes.

As we watched, he climbed onto the metal railing of the walkway.

"I hope Joey doesn't wake all those ducks," Micky said. "They'll make enough noise to bring the security guard out of the building."

"He's stupid enough to get caught," Lisa said. Her voice was angry.

I half turned my head to look at her. *What had this guy ever done to her?*

Lisa saw me turn my head. "If I want to think he's stupid, I can," she told me. "And I can say it, too. Do you have a problem with that?"

Lisa gets into trouble sometimes because of her quick temper. My dad says it's because she's not a happy person. He also says I should look past her temper to see her good side. He's always reminding me that I'm on the baseball team to be a positive role model.

"Nope," I answered Lisa. It was best to keep her good side on my side. "Joey might be stupid. But I'm not."

The frown on her face told me I shouldn't ask her why she disliked the new kid so much. But as far as I could see, all Joey had done was ask how he could join the Sewer Rats.

I thought it would happen the same way I had joined. I'd had to prove myself in a paintball game in the sewers below the streets. Micky and Lisa wanted to know that I wasn't scared of the dark tunnels, that I could be a help to them in the wars.

But Lisa had told Joey that we Sewer Rats proved ourselves in a test at the duck ponds. This test was sneaking inside the fence and balancing on the railing above the slimy water and sleeping ducks.

"Stupid or not," Micky said, watching Joey carefully, "you've got to admit he's got guts."

Joey was in plain view on the walkway. The security guard could notice him any second. His arms were stretched wide as he balanced himself, taking one careful step at a time.

"Guts? I hope he gets caught," Lisa said. "Or, better yet, that he falls in."

I glanced at Lisa and wondered again what Joey had done to make her so mad. He'd only been at school a couple of days. He and his family had just moved to town.

I looked back at Joey.

He had made it halfway across, walking the railing like he was part of a tightrope act.

I looked at the brown slimy water in the pond below him. Brown slimy water with feathers floating in it. Brown slimy water where ducks did a lot more than just paddle. I wondered what would happen if a security guard caught him. I started to get a scared feeling in my stomach, like a ball of spiders wriggling around. The same scared feeling I get every time I go into the tunnels for a paintball war against another team.

Zantor, soldier of the galaxy, I thought silently. *The mighty warrior has removed all emotion as he watches a rookie soldier go up against the alien swamp.*

Mom and Dad have always told me that praying is a good way to deal with fear. But I have my own way. By making this a pretend world, I can make the ball of spiders stop wriggling in my stomach. That's what I do whenever I'm scared—anywhere. In school before a test. Facing down a wild pitcher in a baseball game. And in the dark tunnels beneath the streets. I pretend I am someone else.

You see, scared as I get in the tunnels, there is no

way I can let Micky or Lisa know it. Ever. One, the Sewer Rats are my friends. Two, I need to prove to myself that I can always beat my fear. And three, I don't want a single person in the world to ever know I'm scared.

I stayed in my pretend world and kept watching the new kid.

Zantor smiles. The swamp test provides amusement for the galaxy soldier.

Finally, the spiders of fear in my stomach stopped wriggling.

Lisa stepped back from the fence. Sounds of rustling nylon and a zipper told me she was opening her school backpack. She began to dig through it.

I didn't take my eyes off Joey to see what she was doing.

"What's that?" Micky asked Lisa a few seconds later.

"What's it look like?" she retorted. "A violin?"

Curious, I looked over. Lisa had an airhorn in her hands, the kind that uses pressurized air to make noise. Loud noise. I found out just how loud a second later as it almost shattered my eardrums.

Micky spun and shouted at her. "What are you—"

Lisa cut Micky off by blaring the airhorn again.

I saw Joey stagger a bit on the railing, like he had jumped at the sudden sound.

Lisa blared the airhorn in more short blasts.

Three things happened.

Ducks and geese woke up and added to the noise by quacking, honking, and flapping their wings.

Several people came running, including a big security guard.

And Joey saw the security guard and lost his balance. He dropped into the pond like a giant rock. Then he began to splash in the slimy water like crazy.

"Help!" Joey shouted. "I can't swim. Help! Help!"

He splashed and splashed, even though the pond was only a couple of feet deep.

As the ducks and geese started toward the pond to investigate, Lisa just giggled and giggled.

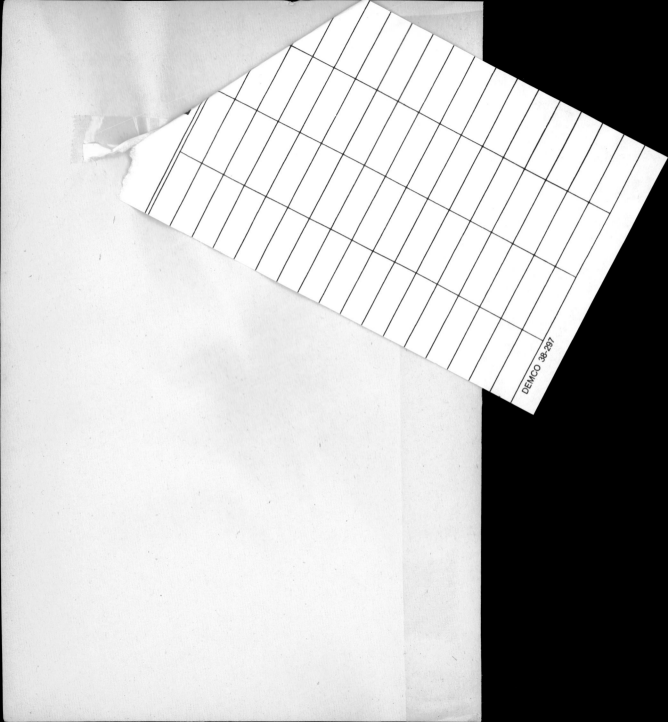